THE CASE OF THE ILL-GOTTEN GOAT

This Large Print Book carries the
Seal of Approval of N.A.V.H.

THE CASE OF THE
ILL-GOTTEN GOAT

CLAUDIA BISHOP

WHEELER PUBLISHING
A part of Gale, Cengage Learning

GALE
CENGAGE Learning·

Detroit • New York • San Francisco • New Haven, Conn • Waterville, Maine • London

GALE
CENGAGE Learning

LIBRARY OF CONGRESS CATALOGING-IN-PUBLICATION DATA

Bishop, Claudia, 1947–
    The case of the ill-gotten goat / by Claudia Bishop.
        p. cm. — (The casebook of Dr. McKenzie series) (Wheeler Publishing large print cozy mystery)
    ISBN-13: 978-1-59722-862-6 (hardcover : alk. paper)
    ISBN-10: 1-59722-862-1 (hardcover : alk. paper)
        1. McKenzie, Austin (Fictitious character)—Fiction.
    2. Veterinarians—Fiction. 3. Murder—Investigation—Fiction.
    4. New York (State)—Fiction. 5. Large type books. I. Title.
    PS3552.I75955C366 2008
    813'.54—dc22   2008035525

Published in 2008 by arrangement with The Berkley Publishing Group, a member of Penguin Group (USA) Inc.

Printed in the United States of America
1 2 3 4 5 6 7 12 11 10 09 08

For Frank Pinkerton, PhD
aka "The Goat Man"

ACKNOWLEDGMENTS

A lot of people tried to help me get it right. My thanks to: Suzanne Messmer of Lively Run Goat Dairies for the tour of a working dairy; Christiane Nussbaumer for the translations into Italian; Tatiana Stanton, PhD, of the Cornell Goat and Sheep Extension Service.

CAST OF CHARACTERS

At McKenzie Veterinary Practice, Inc.
Austin McKenzie, DVM, PhD, professor emeritus
Madeline McKenzie, his wife
Allegra Fulbright, veterinary assistant
Joe Turnblad, veterinary assistant

Citizens of Summersville
Victor Bergland, DVM, PhD, head of the Department of Bovine Sciences
Thelma Bergland, his wife
George and Phyllis Best, owners and operators of Best's Boers
Doucetta Capretti, owner and head cheese maker at the Tre Sorelle Dairy
Marietta Capretti, Doucetta's granddaughter
Frank Celestine, a contractor
Caterina Capretti Celestine, his wife and Doucetta's daughter
Tony and Pietro Celestine, Caterina's sons and Doucetta's grandsons

Neville Brandstetter, PhD, DVM

Anna Luisa Capretti Brandstetter, his wife and Doucetta's daughter

Melvin Staples, a New York state milk inspector

Kelly Staples, his wife

Brian Folk, tax assessor for Summersville

Gordy Rassmussen, town supervisor for Summersville

Mary Ellen Lochmeyer, assistant to the town clerk

Jonathan and Penelope Swinford, owners and operators of Swinford Vineyard

Ashley Swinford, their daughter and a computer expert

Rita Santelli, editor and publisher of the *Summersville Sentinel*

Rudy Schwartz, owner of the Monrovian Embassy diner

Deirdre Franklin, Embassy waitress

Lt. Simon Provost, Summersville Police Department

Kevin Kiddermeister, a policeman

Nigel Fish, a reporter

Leslie Chou, a second-year veterinary student

And Friends

Andrew, a Quarterhorse

Pony, a Shetland pony

Lincoln, a collie
Odie, a house cat
Tracker, a Swedish Warmblood

PROLOGUE

I

"She's, like, a total old bat anyway." Ashley Swinford ran one hand through her blonde hair. Her fingernails were bright red. She'd painted tiny enameled flames on each nail and to Melvin Staples the flames peeking through her tousled curls were a temptation to sin and damnation. She was the daughter of the wealthy vineyard owner Jonathan Swinford, and she'd landed the data entry job at Tre Sorelle Dairy for the summer. That hair and that body were totally beyond Melvin's reach.

"I mean, like, *totally* mean and rotten. Not to mention that she's totally pissed off at *you.* Especially since that new tax assessor's been sniffing around, she's been, like, totally out of control." Ashley leaned across the desk, her blue eyes narrowed, her luscious mouth pursed. "This is, like, the worst possible day you could have picked to come in and check the milk." She sat back and shook her head with a malicious smirk. "I don't know why somebody hasn't run her over with a truck already."

"Hey! You!" Doucetta Capretti marched into the dairy office like a Scud after a weapons depot. A mini Scud, Melvin thought. She can't weigh more than ninety pounds dripping wet. Miserable old bi—

"I seen your car in the drive." Doucetta's birdy black eyes locked onto Melvin's brown ones. A malice-laden smile flickered over her face. She couldn't really read his mind; nobody could know what was in your mind, not if you kept your trap shut and a dirt-eating grin on your face.

"Mrs. C." Melvin stepped away from Ashley's desk and nodded politely. "How've you been?"

"I seen your car in the drive and I ask myself, can this fool be back already?"

Behind him, Ashley gave a pretend cough and messed around with some papers. Melvin had good ears, despite the two years he'd spent in the shrieking chaos of the first war in Iraq. That cough covered a giggle. He kept a tight hold of his temper.

Doucetta thumped her cane on the cement floor. It wasn't the cane of your typical little old lady. It was old, probably older

14

than the ninety-year-old Doucetta herself. The shaft was heavy iron oak. The handle was a big, old brass goat's head, the outlines blurred a little with years of wear. "I call your boss, last time. And I tell him, if you send this arsehole back to test my milk, I send him back to you with a broken head." She thumped so close to him he could smell the garlic she'd had for lunch. "And yet here you are."

"Yes, ma'am."

She hissed, like a snake. "So. Arsehole. You think you're going to find something funny this time? You find something funny in my milk, and you find nothing funny in the milk of those fools down the road?"

"Testing procedure's the same for every-body, ma'am," Melvin said woodenly. "And I couldn't tell you the results of the testing down to Culver's Dairy, ma'am. Besides, they got cows. You've got goats."

"I've got goats," Doucetta said bitterly. "Pft!" She stamped to the heavy door that led to the milk room and hauled it open. "Go in! Test! You'll find all is correct!"

Melvin picked up his testing kit and fol-lowed her inside. The milk room was all concrete, like a bunker: concrete floor, still damp after the morning's sluicing off; concrete walls hung with the hoses that delivered the milk from the milking parlor; concrete ceiling hung with fluorescent lights. The room held three four-hundred-gallon stainless-steel bulk tanks. The Tre Sorelle Dairy milked twice a day, beginning at six in the morning, and again at six at night. The tanks brimmed with the milk collected that morning. A low-pitched rumble assured Melvin that the paddles inside the tanks stirred the contents. The ventilation fans rattled in counterpoint to the sloshing milk.

"You been mixing awhile?" he asked. The rules required at least twenty minutes of mixing before the milk was tested. You went by the book with Doucetta.

Doucetta shrugged. Melvin'd seen all three parts of *The Godfather* movies, and he wasn't surprised that Doucetta always wore black. That was what old Italian ladies did. Black blouse, draggy black skirt, and a ratty black sweater, despite the fact that it was mid-August and ninety degrees in the shade. "A hour, maybe more," she said. "Go. Do your test. Arsehole."

Melvin set his kit on the floor. He carried his long stainless-steel testing ladle in a tall, skinny jar filled with a bleach solution. He removed the ladle and held it up to let it dry in the draft from the fans. Then he unlatched the top of the tank nearest the door and heaved it open. The milk swirled in the tank, releasing a warm, almost yeasty scent into the air. Melvin lowered the ladle carefully into the bluish white depths, raised it carefully, and stepped back. Doucetta darted forward and slammed the heavy cover shut. Melvin poured the milk sample into a sterile specimen jar, capped it, and placed it inside a heavy plastic bag, which he sealed with tape. He wrote the date, time, and location on the bag and put it in his kit.

"That milk is good milk," Doucetta said. She had maybe a million wrinkles and they all folded together as she directed a malignant glare at him. "That milk is good milk, and if your tests say it is not, it is because you have peed in the sample, perhaps. This test comes back no good, I'll get your job yet. Arsehole."

Melvin nodded politely. "Ma'am." He pulled open the heavy door to the office and made his way past the luscious Ashley to his van outside. As he pulled down the driveway, Doucetta shook her cane in the air and shrieked after him: "Arsehole!"

II

"We've got to do something, Frank, or she's going to bankrupt us all." Caterina held the

17

kitchen drape slightly aside and peered out the window at her mother and Melvin Staples. The milk inspector got into his van and pulled the driver's door closed with the carefully controlled movements of a man about to blow. Caterina watched Doucetta's mouth move in silent imprecation. "She's calling him a pile of names," Caterina said over her shoulder. "You can just tell. If she doesn't ease up, I don't know what's going to happen to us all. I told you about the tax assessor's visit, didn't I? She almost took the guy's head off with that cane. And the language!"

"So?" her husband said indifferently. Frank Celestine sat at the long cherry kitchen table, in front of a tuna sandwich. He wore a gray cotton T-shirt with Celestine Builders and his name stitched on the chest pocket. Frank owned two dozen of them. Every morning Caterina set out a clean dress shirt for Frank to wear, and every morning he pulled on a Celestine Builders gray cotton T-shirt. After thirty-five years, she knew Frank figured that she'd give it up. She hadn't yet. He shoveled the remains of his lunch into his mouth, and then swallowed. "She insults everybody. Forget about it."

Caterina watched as her mother waved her

cane over her head, then slammed it cane-point down on the concrete step in front of the dairy office door. Then the old lady went back into the office and banged the door so hard the OPEN sign bounced.

From this vantage point, Caterina could see all the way down the drive to Route 333. The taillights of the milk inspector's van flashed briefly red as he stopped before pulling out into traffic. He turned left and disappeared from Caterina's sight.

"You want me to forget about it? You'll be sorry that you wanted me to forget about it when we end up homeless on the street." She let the drapes close, pressed her forefingers into her temples, and shut her eyes. "If the somatic cell count comes back too high this time, we're in for it."

Frank grunted. It was a bored, yeah-yeah-yeah-whatever grunt, as opposed to an actively hostile don't-bother-me grunt. Mildly encouraged, Caterina continued: "This would make three times in a row we've missed the target, Frank. And you know what that means." She crossed the kitchen and sat down opposite him. Frank cut into the sour cream coffee cake she'd made that morning, and then held the slice aloft. He looked at it in a considering way, then bit into it. "The state will bring in the people from Cornell and they'll be poking their noses all over the dairy. Mamma will pitch a fit. Frank? Are you listening to me? We need to talk to her. All of us, Anna Luisa, Marietta, and you, too."

"Yeah? Fat lot of good that's going to do you. She'll just call you a fat dumb *vacca,* and you'll cry . . ." Here he screwed one knuckle into his eye and went "boo-hoo-hoo" in a high, effeminate voice. "And Anna Luisa will screech like a crow and Marietta will look down that long nose of hers at the lot of you, and you'll end up looking dumber than you already are."

"Somebody's got to pay attention to what's going on," Caterina said with soft stubbornness.

Frank shoved himself away from the table. "You know what you should pay attention to?" He leaned over her and patted her shoulder, too hard. "You oughta forget about making that coffee cake six times a week. You quit making that coffee cake, you might get rid of some of that extra flab." He pinched her upper arm, and she winced. He straightened his shoulders.

There were several reasons why Frank wore his Celestine Builders T-shirts every day. One was to let people think he ran his own business and that he didn't live off the money from her mother's dairy. (A lie. And a big one.) Another was Frank thought he was in pretty good shape and the T-shirt let people know that, too. That wasn't so much of a lie. He spent a lot of time at the Summersville Country Club alternating between the bar and the gym.

Frank headed toward the back door, shoulders back, belly sucked in.

Caterina tried to keep the high note of worry out of her voice. "Where are you going?"

"Gotta see a guy about a job."

Caterina couldn't help herself. "What job? Where?"

"Just butt out, will ya?"

The door slammed behind him.

She got to her feet, picked up Frank's dirty dishes, and took them to the sink. The kitchen had a dishwasher, two of them, in fact, but she filled the sink with hot, soapy water and began the ritual of washing up. She loved this kitchen, loved baking in it, eating in it, cleaning up in it. She had a sixty-inch dual-fuel Viking range. A forty-eight-inch Viking refrigerator. The tiles on the floor were handmade, sent all the way over to Summersville, New York, from Mamma's old village in Tuscany. The granite countertops were bevel-edged, with fleurde-lys carved in each corner. And the dishes she washed with such love and attention were Rosenthal china.

Caterina discovered she was crying into the sink.

And it was all the milk inspector's fault.

III

"I can't imagine living like this," gushed the woman from New York. "It's paradise."

Marietta kept her smile carefully in place. She'd been keeping the smile in place all morning long. Tuesdays were tour days at the Tre Sorelle Dairy and in August, the tours overflowed with skinny, condescending urban professionals in trendy Tod's and shriekingly expensive little linen shifts. June tours meant a lot of schoolkids with sticky fingers and earsplitting shouts. July was young families with barfing toddlers. August was urban refugees like this particular woman; a stockbroker, she'd informed Marietta just once too often. September meant retirees, who at least got tired sooner rather than later.

All of them got up her nose.

Marietta flexed the left rein and Peter the Percheron obligingly hawed to the left, bumping the tour wagon over a large pothole. The stockbroker yelled, "Ow!" and looked daggers.

"Those of you on a first visit to the Finger Lakes may want to know why this region carries the name." Marietta pulled Peter to a halt. She gestured at the lake spreading its glories before them. "There are five large freshwater lakes here in upstate New York, and on the map, the lakes look like a hand." She held up her hand, palm flat, fingers outspread. She wriggled her middle finger. "We're overlooking Cayuga, which is between Keuka and Seneca. The water is that deep, lucid blue because of the glaciers that moved through this part of the continent millions of years ago."

There was an appreciative murmur from the fifteen people jammed into the farm wagon.

"Most of you know that Tompkins County is wine country, of course. Our whites in particular have an international reputation. And we are gaining a reputation for our goat cheese, as well." Marietta turned from the lake to the acres of Tre Sorelle behind them. The barns that housed the dairy herd formed a U at the top of a long, thickly grassed pasture surrounded by white fences. The dairy, the office, and the produce shop formed another U around a bricked courtyard with a fountain in the middle and a latticework roof draped with blooming wisteria. The ground rose on the opposite side of the driveway to a sprawling house. "And I am proud to say that Tre Sorelle cheeses are at the forefront of the industry."

"Tre Sorelle means 'three sisters' in English," the man who accompanied the stockbroker said officiously. He wore flip-flops, designer jeans that Marietta knew started at five hundred dollars a pair, and sunglasses so expensive she had no idea who made them. He gestured at the Tre Sorelle logo emblazoned on the barn — three pretty brunettes with gold hoop earrings and head scarves tied jauntily around their curls. "I take it you're one of the three? Do you milk the goats between tours?"

"And when did you and your sisters come to this country?" the stockbroker asked.

Marietta would have bet her quarterly share of the dairy proceeds that the guy was a lawyer. Probably from some white-shoe firm near Wall Street. Her second husband had been a lawyer. She'd hated the entire profession ever since the satisfyingly nasty divorce. Her first husband had been a stockbroker. She'd met him during her internship with Bear Stearns. She hated stockbrokers, too.

She dimpled attractively at both of them

and adjusted the Tre Sorelle head scarf her grandmother made them all wear when dealing with the public. "My grandmother first came to America as a sixteen-year-old in 1929," she said. "And she had three daughters with Grandpapa Dominic. My mother was one of the three. Her name was Margarita. Mamma passed away four years ago. Her sisters are still alive of course. I have two aunties — Anna Luisa and Caterina. Grandmamma never really got over Mamma's death so I took her place — or try to at least. So there are still *tre* sorelle. Me, Anna Luisa, and Caterina."

"And you all live together in that beautiful house?" someone in the back said incredulously.

Marietta's smile tightened. "Yes, we do."

"You told us at the outset of the tour that your grandmother still runs the dairy," Stockbroker said with a dubious kind of sneer. "If she came here in 1929, she's how old?"

"Ninety-four." Marietta settled her gold hoop earring more firmly into her earlobe.

"And she's not . . . ?" Stockbroker whirled her finger expressively around her ear.

"Sharp as a tack," Marietta said cheerfully.

"So, you and your aunts and your ninety-

25

four-year-old grandmother run the place?"
The lawyer looked impressed.

"We have a resident herd manager. And
two full-time assistants. But my grandmother still makes a lot of the cheese
herself." She shook the reins and Pete the
Percheron broke into an obliging amble.
Could she drive them all into the lake and
let them drown, screaming bloody murder?
Nope. Grandmamma would have her guts
for garters. And she couldn't risk that. Not
now. Not until Grandmamma coughed up
enough money to take care of Marietta's
more pressing bills.

Which shouldn't be a problem as long as
the taxes stayed down and the flippin'
somatic cell count came in under a million
this time.

Marietta cracked the whip viciously in the
air. She just might have to have a little one-
on-one with that milk inspector.

IV

Neville Brandstetter slouched back in his
all-leather executive 5000 model easy chair
and swung his feet onto the highest stack of
paper on his desk. The topmost set of
papers shifted. Leslie Chou winced, but the
papers held under Neville's worn Docksid-
ers.

"Anyhow," she said, "I think we should send the quality team out to Tre Sorelle no matter what the MSCC is this time."

"Has the third sample from Tre Sorelle come back from the lab yet?"

She shook her head. "Mel went out to draw it this morning at ten." She checked her watch. "He'll have FedEx'd it to Albany by now. We'll get the results tomorrow afternoon. But this is a really interesting case, Dr. Brandstetter. Nobody knows why the count keeps coming back over a million. It'd be different if the place were a slum. But it's not. I took one of the tours earlier this summer, you know. The place is as clean as a whistle. It's gorgeous. Whatever's sending the somatic cell count up, it's not an everyday cleanliness issue." She pushed her wire-rimmed spectacles up her nose and grinned hopefully at him.

Neville sighed. He liked Leslie. She was one of the brighter second-years in Cornell's vet program. And unlike a lot of his students, she wasn't attracted to the glamourous side of the profession. Leslie liked horses, had an easy affection for cats and dogs and a grave appreciation for cows and swine — but she loved goats.

"You're thinking you can maybe get a paper out of this for the small ruminants class," he guessed.

She beamed. Leslie was thirty pounds overweight, her soft black hair refused to stay in her ponytail, and she had the appealing clumsiness of a puppy. Neville found her irresistible, in his heavily paternal way. "Getting a paper out of it would be the nuts," she admitted. "But who's to say? If nothing else, I can get a better grip on how a really fabulous dairy's run. And Mrs. Capretti's practically a legend! I mean, I'm just dying to meet her. You've known her for years, I bet."

Neville knew Doucetta Capretti, all right. Although anyone who had anything to do with goats within a five-hundred-mile radius of his very comfortable office knew Doucetta, he had a better reason. "She's my mother-in-law," he said dryly. "To be precise, soon to be my ex-mother-in-law."

Leslie blinked at him and skipped right over the reference to his marriage. "You mean Mrs. Brandstetter was brought up with goats? Is that totally cool, or what?"

Anna Luisa hated goats. Almost as much as she hated Neville Brandstetter. But not quite.

"Anna Luisa has as little to do with the dairy as possible."

Leslie's disbelief was palpable. "Gosh.

That's like, so sad. Anyway. I've never been on a quality process call. I think it'll be exciting, getting to know a dairy from the inside out."

Neville could think of a few things more exciting than Doucetta's response to a bunch of academics poking their collective noses in her business. A third Gulf War, maybe. He swung his feet to the floor and leaned forward. "You'd need a mentor to go in with you, Leslie. The department's stretched pretty thin at the moment. I don't have a goat man . . . sorry, or woman . . . that can take the time to supervise."

Leslie's big brown eyes looked appealingly into his. "Oh, Dr. Neville. There must be *somebody*."

There were, in fact, two professors who would be ideal mentors and who liked Leslie as much as everybody else did. On the other hand, both of them knew Doucetta all too well. Neville sighed with real regret. "I'm afraid this one's not —"

"And it doesn't have to be a goat specialist, necessarily, does it?" Leslie interrupted eagerly. "I mean, as long as it's a full professor, it'd be okay, wouldn't it?" She sighed wistfully. "There must be *somebody*."

Well, there was, in fact, somebody.

Neville shook his head. Nah. It'd be a

disaster.

On the other hand, it wouldn't be a department disaster, and as long as nobody quit . . . He thought about it. Considering the personalities involved, nobody innocent was going to get hurt. He chuckled, and for a moment, his depression over the state of his marriage lifted. Then he said, "Maybe. Maybe there is. Tell you what, Leslie. I'll talk to Victor Bergland and see what he can do."

Leslie's smile would have made cherubs sing and angels cluck approvingly. Neville could see what she was thinking: Dr. Bergland was department chair. If anyone could find a kindly mentor, it was Dr. Bergland.

V

"The thing is, Mel, the county's plain flat broke." Brian Folk emphasized the "flat broke" with the flat of his hand on the dashboard of Melvin Staples's car. "You got your basic good citizens like you and me paying taxes through the nose for the houses that we bust our butts to pay for, and then you got the fat-cat businesses that squirm out of paying their fair share and what d'ya got?"

"My job's on the line here," Mel said. "The old bat's after my job as it is."

30

"I say, what d'ya got?" Brian asked rhetorically. The Summersville Board of Supervisors had appointed him tax assessor for a dang good reason. Nobody pushed Brian Folk around. Not the least some ninety-year-old biddy with a mean mouth. "You got unfairness, that's what you've got. You got inequity." He held up a sample jar filled with bluish milk. "And here, you got goat's milk with a guaranteed — what d'ya call it?"

"Somatic cell count," Melvin said. "It's a reading of the number of white blood cells that have been sloughed off in raw milk."

"Whatever," Brian Folk said. "That sample you took from Tre Sorelle comes back with, say, a zillion of those little babies . . ."

"A million," Melvin said. "That's the standard for goats. And I'll tell you something, Brian, it's a dang stupid standard. Goats naturally shed more white blood cells than cows, or sheep, even. They have a naturally higher count, and when I don't want to wring the old bat's neck for her, I can see she's got a point. There's probably nothing basically wrong with the milk."

Brian didn't need to hear anything more than Mel's last sentence. "See? So what's to hurt? The dang milk's fine."

"But it might not be," Melvin said. "The state sets that standard because it means something, see? I fake that result, somebody might end up sicker than a dog from drinking the stuff and like I said, my job's on the line."

"So let's say you send in that sample you just got and the count comes back a zillion . . ."

"Over a million," Melvin said.

Brian sighed theatrically. Melvin didn't seem to be getting the picture. "And then what? The dairy gets shut down, 'cause it's three times and you're out, right?"

"Not necessarily. Like I told you, the state and the school send in a team to look stuff over."

"Whatever. It's going to play holy hollyhocks with the fair market value, right? And I do my assessment of fair market value based on how much that place is worth, and if they got this problem, it ends up being worth a pile of dog doo-doo, don't it?"

Melvin shrugged.

"And the old bat goes to plead this nice fat assessment I got for her." Brian smoothed the folder in his lap with pleasure. "And she's got, maybe a leg to stand on."

Melvin rubbed his hand across his forehead.

"So her taxes go way down, and *then,* you end up losing your job anyhow, right? 'Cause the county's broke and phhft!" He snapped his fingers. "They don't have enough to pay your salary."

Melvin didn't seem to be following this carefully thought-out logic. He stared through the windshield at the sunny August day outside, his face blank. His brain's a blank, too, Brian thought, thanks very much. There was more than one dim bulb in Melvin Staples's chandelier or he wouldn't have listened to any of this crapola in the first place.

"Looky here." Brian set the flask of guaranteed legal SCC goat's milk on the seat between them. "I'm just going to leave this little bottle here, just like that. You drive yourself on down to the FedEx office and you think about what I told you all the way." He patted Melvin on the shoulder. "And I can count on you to do the right thing, Melvin."

Brian slid out of Melvin's van and closed the passenger-side door softly. He'd arranged a pretty good meeting spot. The parking lot behind the Summersville High School was totally dead in August. He got into his Chevy Caprice, waited until Melvin pulled out of the parking lot, and turned right onto Main Street. Well, that was one iron in the fire that might work out to his advantage. He was a patient man. A man who took his time about things. The assessment was only one nail in the old biddy's coffin. He'd make dang sure there were a couple more.

ONE

My wife bumped open the French door to our terrace and backed onto the porch. She held a bottle of Scotch in one hand and a tea tray in the other. It was a vision that inspired me to recite aloud the words of that most sensuous of poets, Omar Khayyam:

"A loaf of bread
a jug of wine and thou
beside me in the wilderness.
Ah! This were paradise enow!"

The collie at my feet gave an approving woof.

"It's just me and a bit of a snack, Austin." Madeline gave me a kiss. Then she beamed at an envelope propped between the plate of Parmesan-dusted cheese puffs and a plate of grape tomatoes from our garden. "And the check from the police department!"

She set the loaded tray on the table at my elbow, sank gracefully into the chair opposite mine, and seized the envelope with every appearance of satisfaction.

It was my favorite time of day at the offices of McKenzie Veterinary Practice, Inc. (Practice limited to large animals). After a successful afternoon castrating bull calves, we were more than ready for our usual four o'clock respite. The sun was setting in a blaze of color not too far removed from the glory of my wife's auburn hair. My collie Lincoln was at my feet. My beloved was at my side. We were meeting our old friends the Berglands in a few hours for a Friday night fish fry. Peace buzzed like a bee around the green acres of our farm.

I poured a large glass of Scotch and took a satisfying sip. "Ah!" I said. "This is indeed the life!"

Few would have guessed that not more than a year ago, I had been in a state of gloom over the state of our finances. After a long and happy career as the chair of Bovine Sciences at the nearby veterinary school, I had retired to a life of ease and comfort with my wife, my dog, and my horses. But a careless foray into the world of high finance had made a hash of our retirement income. I had, perforce, opened a veterinary practice to keep the wolf from the door and food on the table. While not precisely prospering, our clinic did well enough that we recruited two assistants along the way. But, to the amazement of those who know me well, it is not my clinic practice that keeps New York State Electric and Gas a happy provider to the McKenzie household; it is our newly hatched detective agency, Cases Closed.

"Hm," Madeline said, after a close perusal of the check. "Simon warned me that it might take a while for the village council to approve the check, but this is speedy, Austin. I sent the invoice for the O'Leary case in just last week."

"Simon was undoubtedly grateful for the dispatch with which we cornered the murderer," I said with no small sense of satisfaction. Simon Provost, Summersville's chief of detectives, is a good man to have on one's side in the detection business.

"It's more likely he wants the whole thing over and done with and you . . . I mean us . . . out of his hair." Madeline tucked the check in the pocket of her denim skirt, leaned over the end table, and kissed me again. "Rita said the sales of the *Sentinel* doubled the weeks she was covering the case. And Becky Provost said Simon's acid reflux was so bad the whole month of July that she was going to send the bill for those stomach tablets to the CNN news desk in Syracuse. The reporters just didn't let up on him. I don't know why everyone finds murder so fascinatin', but they surely seemed to in this case."

In moments of slight stress, my wife's southern origins can be found in the number of dropped *g*'s in her speech.

"I suppose it's just good old human nature." She reached over and helped herself to a substantial number of cheese puffs. "And it's surely satisfyin' to see a murderer collared and sent off to the pokey. Not to mention that the detective business has added a good bit to our bottom line." She sat back, her sapphire eyes reflective. "On the other hand, it's a sorry state of affairs, Austin, when the bills get paid because some poor soul's bought the farm. But the checking account's low. We need another murder." She dispatched the cheese puffs with a sigh.

I was at a loss for a response, so I picked up a cheese puff and ate it. My wife is both an enthusiastic eater and a notable cook. It was an excellent cheese puff, so I had another.

"Of course, if you want a good candidate

for our next corpse, I've got one," Madeline said. Her sapphire eyes darkened a trifle.

I raised one eyebrow in query. Madeline is of a genial and easygoing disposition. Animus of this type is most unlike her.

"Thelma Bergland, that's who," Madeline responded, although I hadn't actually asked the question. "Ever since Thelma inherited that pile from her rich old auntie, she's been drivin' us all to distraction. You know how Lila and I have our usual Friday lunch? Thelma called up yesterday, asked if she could join us, and she didn't show. Didn't even call. So we went and ate without her." Another cheese puff disappeared down Madeline's throat. "Phooey."

"Thelma came into an inheritance?" I said.

"Austin, sometimes I think you don't listen to a thing I say. I told you all about it last night after supper."

I had spent the prior evening writing a draft of my weekly column for the *Summersville Sentinel,* Ask Dr. McKenzie! (The exclamation mark is courtesy of the *Sentinel's* advertising department.) The issue at hand had been a particularly interesting question about sarcoptic mange. I had a faint recollection of hearing Madeline's mellow contralto murmuring in the background. Clearly, I'd missed news of some import.

"So you did," I said cordially. "But I hadn't realized a small legacy would make that much of a change in their circumstances."

"Small legacy? Austin, it was two and a half million dollars!"

"Good heavens," I said. I was astonished into momentary silence. Then, as my surprise abated, "Well, good for them." Victor, who had succeeded me as chair of the Bovine Sciences department, had long wanted to establish a Bergland bovine scholarship fund. Now he'd be able to do it.

Madeline sipped her iced tea and gazed over the porch railing at the ducklings bobbing on the pond at the foot of the lawn. A pair of Muscovy ducks had taken up residence there this spring. The two were on their second family. "Austin. What's the first thing we'd do if somebody dropped two and a half million dollars in our laps?"

"Raise Allegra's and Joe's salary." Although there was only one full-time job available at our clinic, Madeline and I had been unable to decide between the two applicants who had showed up to interview for the position. So the two of them shared the job, for not much more than a pittance, I'm sorry to say.

"And then what?"

I was stumped.

"We'd get a dishwasher."

"And then what?"

I have to admit that other than the comfort of knowing that the taxes and utility bills would be covered every month, there's only one thing we wanted that cost anywhere near two and half million dollars.

"The McKenzie Medal for Outstanding Research in Bovine Sciences," Madeline said, with her usual perceptiveness. She placed her warm hand on my mine. I clasped it affectionately. "Not to mention that program where you can buy a goat for a third world family. Oh, there's a lot of useful stuff we could do with that kind of cash."

"But what would *you* do with it, my dear?"

"We have everything we want. I mean, I'd be just as happy if NYSEG put us back on their Christmas card list, but we're going to be payin' those bills on time for the rest of this year, at least, so I'm not really worried about that."

"I should point out that the money has been left to the Berglands, and not the two of us," I said. "Perhaps we should curb these flights of fancy. Just what is Thelma up to?"

Through the open windows behind me, I heard the phone ring. I ignored it. There are few things in life more intrusive than the telephone; there is *nothing* more intrusive than the telephone's obnoxious younger cousin, the cell phone.

"Thelma?" Madeline began as she rose to her feet, "Thelma is . . . well. You'll just have to see for yourself at dinner tonight." She disappeared through the French doors to our living room, and reappeared moments later, the telephone receiver in her hand. "It's for you, darlin'." Then, as she handed the receiver to me she mouthed, *Victor.*

I held the phone in my hand for a moment. What should one say to a legatee, especially one who had suddenly, unexpectedly, come into a large quantity of cash? A legatee, moreover, who was a friend of long standing? Perhaps a quiet but heartfelt "Congratulations" was in order. I put the phone to my ear and said, "McKenzie here."

"Austin, it's good to hear your voice. How are you?" my old friend said courteously.

Victor's usual greeting is over-hearty, profane, and insulting. Somewhat taken aback, I said, "I'm well, Victor. And you?"

"As well as can be expected."

This, then, was the moment to offer a

modest "Well done!" or "Delighted to hear of your good fortune." I drew breath.

"Is this a convenient time?" he rolled on, smoothly.

"It's four fifteen in the afternoon," I said. "You know perfectly well I'm drinking Scotch."

"Of course. Sorry to trouble you. Perhaps I could call you later."

This was all extremely unsettling. By now, Victor and I should have exchanged rude opinions on our intelligences at the very least. "No, no. Please. Go ahead."

"I have a favor to ask."

"Certainly."

"Neville Brandstetter has a young second-year, Leslie Chou."

Brandstetter I knew. Very sound in anything pertaining to goats. "The student doesn't come to mind, but I know Brandstetter, of course." A bit of a joker, I recalled. And he was the possessor of a large red beard that must plague him no end in this heat.

"He's come up short on a QMPS team. Needs an experienced veterinary to supervise young Chou. Shouldn't take more than a few weeks of your time, if that. And there's a stipend attached, of course."

A Quality Milk Production Services team

partners with the State of New York to assess the suitability of working processes of dairies. The team consists of a veterinarian and several technicians. The former is usually a professor in good standing at the ag school. The latter can be students or those trained in various aspects of the milk trade: nutrition, chemistry, whatever. I am a beef man, myself, although I have more than a passing acquaintance with dairy cattle. A thought occurred to me. "Brandstetter's goats."

"True."

"You want me to supervise a quality team at a goat dairy?" I was nonplussed. I treat very few goats — just George and Phyllis Best of Best's Boers — none of them dairy.

"The girl's quite knowledgeable. And how complicated can it be, Austin? The milking process is the same whether it's cows or pygmy buffalo." This isn't strictly true, of course, since the chemistry of milk varies considerably between species, but I was relieved to hear the testiness. That was a bit of the old Victor!

"Not very," I admitted. "I'll need to brush up on the sampling procedures. And I know next to nothing about the periods of normal changes in the milk due to lactation."

"Please add whatever research time you

44

need to the invoice," Victor said. "So I can tell Brandstetter you've agreed? He asked for you specifically, for some reason."

Odder still. But an invoice was an invoice. "Certainly." I had a sudden, unwelcome thought. "It wouldn't be Tre Sorelle dairy, by any chance?"

Victor paused.

"Anna Luisa's dairy. His wife," I added, by way of clarification. "Who is the daughter of that notorious termagant, Doucetta Capretti."

"It is, Austin, but . . ."

"There's no 'perhaps' about it," I said. "The answer is no, Victor."

"Are you sure?" he asked with concern. "I know how tight things are for you folks and I thought . . ."

"The detective business is shaping up nicely," I said rather icily. "And the clinic business is substantially improved. I would rather spend a week at a shopping mall than one second overseeing Ms. Capretti's goats. The elder Ms. Capretti, to be precise." Her granddaughter Marietta Capretti was quite a dish. So was Anna Luisa.

"If you're sure," Victor said doubtfully.

"I am certain."

"Neville will be disappointed. But I'll let him know. And, oh, Austin?"

"Still here, Victor," I said impatiently.

"There's been a change in plans for tonight's dinner."

Our standing date for the Friday night fish fry was at the Monrovian Embassy, Summersville's best hamburger joint. "Oh, yes?"

"Thelma thought we'd enjoy an evening at Suzanne's."

"Suzanne's?" This restaurant made the food at the Inn at Hemlock Falls look paltry! The Sunday edition of the *New York Times* had called it a gourmet experience to be savored again and again. This was a far cry from the beer-battered onions of the Embassy. I glanced at Madeline. She frowned. I rarely see my wife frown. She extended her hand for the phone.

"Victor? Are you two thinkin' we might go to Suzanne's tonight instead of the Embassy? You are? Would it be okay with you if we saved Suzanne's for another time? I'd need a little more time to prepare for a place that nice. You understand? Great. Thank you, darlin'. We'll see you at the usual time." Madeline clicked the phone off and held it in her hand as if judging its weight. "Suzanne's," she said. "As if. And it's forty dollars an entrée. Whooee."

And that, until we sat at the Monrovian

Embassy with the Berglands, was her entire comment on the matter of Thelma's two-and-a-half-million-dollar inheritance.

The Monrovian Embassy is a byword in Summersville. Rudy Schwartz's breakfasts are close to incomparable; nowhere else will one find such crisp hash browns, such smoky-flavored bacon. At lunch and dinner, the Monrovian hamburger smothered in beer-battered onion rings is second to none. But it is the Friday night fish fry that brings Summersvillians out in force. It is fortunate indeed that Rudy's steers are regular clients of the McKenzie clinic; we would have trouble getting a table otherwise.

The Embassy sits on Main Street; the rear parking lot is on the edge of a small tributary to Cayuga Lake. At quarter to seven, I parked our Bronco near the Dumpster, the scene of the crime in our recently closed murder case. "That brings up memories," I said, gazing at the rusty metal sides with some affection.

"And what does that bring up?" Madeline said with unaccustomed tartness. "Your breakfast, I bet." I followed the direction of her forefinger. An enormous red Hummer sat on the grass verge between the parking lot and the stream. It was trimmed in brass:

brass bumpers, brass surrounds on the headlights, brass handles on the doors.

"Victor's?" I said in some surprise.

"Thelma's auntie didn't leave her millions to Victor," Madeline said. "It's Thelma's."

Although Thelma is shaped like an artichoke and has the voice of a mandrill monkey, she is a sound liberal. A Democrat you can count on. The Hummer was an anomaly of no small order.

We made our way through the crowd at the front door and into the belly of the restaurant itself. The interior — like the shambling exterior — is comfortably shabby. Battered wooden booths line one wall; a long wooden bar lines the other. The middle is occupied by a higgledy-piggledy collection of tables and chairs. The back wall has three doors: one on each side leads to the bathrooms; the center goes into the kitchen.

Victor sat in our regular booth, the one nearest the Gents. He rose and waved us on. Thelma was next to him; I didn't see all of her until I sat down next to Madeline.

"Good heavens," I said. "What happened to you, Thelma?"

My wife put her hand on my knee and pinched it.

"Howdy, Thelma," Madeline said cheerfully. "Lila and I missed seein' you at lunch today."

"I spent most of the day in Syracuse," Thelma said. "Shopping."

I wondered what store had exploded over Thelma's person — although I didn't say that aloud.

Madeline tells me one can infer a number of things about human beings from they way they look. She has a point. Exterior clues can reveal many things about health. A staring coat can be evidence of malnutrition or parasite infestation. A dull hide or a shelly hoof may indicate an endocrine imbalance. A generally unkempt appearance has a lot to say about the responsibility of one's caretaker.

We've known Thelma Bergland for more than twenty years, and she's always looked like an artichoke. She didn't resemble an artichoke anymore. Something had pinched her figure in, in places where formerly it had bulged out. Her hair was a bright yellow instead of liver brown. She had a lot of stuff on her face. Glittery blue stuff on her eyelids. Pink stuff on her cheeks. She clanked when she moved, due, I assumed, to the amount of gold jewelry on her bosom and wrists.

"So, Austin," Victor said, rather loudly.

"Have you changed your mind about Neville Brandstetter's offer yet? He's anxious that somebody gets a look in at the dairy. Seems the somatic cell count keeps coming back well over a million."

"Have I what? No," I said rather testily. "I haven't." I stopped looking at Thelma and looked at Victor. His somewhat stocky self was stuffed into a sports coat. His hair was shorter and glistened with something very like Show Sheen. With his banana-shaped nose and wooly hair, Victor always reminds me of a Suffolk ram; at the moment, he looked more sheepish than usual.

"See something funny?" he asked in rather a dangerous way.

This new Victor would not appreciate my little pun, so I said, "Not at all." Then taking the ram by the horns, so to speak, I said, "I understand congratulations are in order. I hear you've come into a bit of a windfall."

"Well, of course," Thelma said in her corvine screech — at least her voice hadn't mutated into something strange and wonderful! — "it's *my* 'windfall' as you call it. Victor didn't get a penny." She withdrew a handkerchief from her handbag and dabbed at each eye. I was curious to see if the glittery blue stuff rubbed off. It didn't. "My poor aunt Violet. Such a loss." She tucked the cloth back in her bag and snapped, "Victor, would you *please* check on our drinks? We put our order in ages ago."

"Of course, dear." Victor got up and headed toward the bar.

"Victor!" Thelma said.

He stopped halfway there, shook his head as if he had a fly in his ear, and came back.

"Austin and Madeline would like something, too, I'm sure." She smiled. There was a bit of red stuff on her teeth. Her teeth looked a lot whiter than they had before. And more pointed, somehow, although that may have been my imagination. "Please. Order what you like, you two. It's on me."

"Scotch for you, old man," Victor said heartily. "Maddy? What about you?"

Thelma tapped her glass with a fingernail. Her fingernails had grown a lot longer in the week since I'd seen her last. This was puzzling. "Try a Campari and soda, Madeline. It's delicious."

"Thank you," Madeline said. "That sounds just fine."

Victor bumbled off to the bar.

"Thelma," I said, "your appearance has changed. What . . ." Madeline's warm hand tightened warningly on my knee.

I subsided into sheer confusion for the rest of the evening.

■ ■ ■ ■

"Thelma inherits two and a half million dollars and Dr. Bergland ends up putting Show Sheen in his hair?" Allegra said gleefully. "Oh. My. Goodness." She burst into giggles. Allegra's giggle is infectious, and the rest of us around the breakfast table couldn't help but smile. She is a pretty girl, with greenish eyes and hair the color of a Hershey bar. She was about to enter her first year as a veterinary student and was preparing by taking a few summer courses in small animal husbandry.

"That's not what it's all about, though, is it?" Joe said. Joe, about to enter his third year as a veterinary student, just manages to keep afloat with a combination of scholarships, our clinic salary, and an occasional odd job as bartender at the Monrovian Embassy. His shift at the Embassy had started at nine last night, just as Madeline and I were leaving. He'd started his breakfast by regaling Allegra with tales of Thelma's behavior. "Bossed him around, buying exotic drinks for anyone they even knew remotely. Rudy doesn't stock half the stuff she asked for. She's using the money to beat poor Doc Bergland over the head."

He hunched disapprovingly over his oatmeal. "It's pretty brutal."

"Well, I'm sure they'll work it out just fine," Madeline said.

Saturdays are less frenetic than weekdays, and we begin breakfast at nine, rather than the usual seven o'clock, which meant the mail had been delivered. Madeline sorted through the stack and said somewhat absently, "Getting that kind of money dumped in your lap all of a sudden is like being out in a storm in a tippy boat. Hard to keep your balance."

Allegra's laughter deserted her abruptly. "Money," she said darkly. Her own family had nearly been destroyed by her father's pursuit of it. Sam Fulbright had paid the price — one to three years in a downstate prison — but Allegra still dealt with the aftermath. Thanks to a legacy from her grandmother, her own studies at Cornell were paid for, but she needed her assistant's pay to supplement it. "She's going to be sorry she ever cashed that check."

Madeline, perusing a letter, said, "Ally, honey, it's no use fretting over stuff like money . . . good glory!"

In twenty-two years of happily married life, I'd never heard that tone of voice from my wife before. Joe half rose out of his chair.

Lincoln began to bark. Juno, our half-bred Akita, chased her tail in an agony of excitement. Even Odie the cat stopped her methodical tail washing and stared at us, her gold eyes wide.

"My dear, whatever is the matter?"

"Taxes!" Madeline smacked the letter flat on the table. "It's this year's bill for taxes!"

I settled back in my chair. Lincoln looked at me, yawned, and curled himself at my feet. Odie abruptly resumed the ministrations to her tail. Only the people in the room remained attentive. "I had heard we were due to be reassessed," I said. "I take it the news is not hopeful?"

"You know what's not going to be hopeful? That tax assessor's future ability to bear children, that's what's not going to be hopeful." Madeline's eyes are a deep sapphire; when she is irked, they turn navy blue. On these very rare occasions, it's wise to give the woman room to breathe.

Joe and Allegra exchanged glances. "Well," Allegra said brightly, "I'm off duty today, so I think I'll go out and school Tracker for a bit."

"And since we've got a barn call to make, maybe we'd better get a move on, Doc." Joe shoved himself to his feet and began to clear the table.

"Excellent idea, my boy," I said. "Unless, my dear, you need me here to fight the good fight for you?"

"Oh, no, darlin'," Madeline said with an exceptionally sweet smile. "I'm takin' care of this myself!"

Two

At some time during the course of our first farm call that morning, a person or persons unknown coshed Melvin Staples, the milk inspector, over the head and dumped the body into the four-hundred-gallon bulk tank at the Tre Sorelle Dairy.

I was not to discover this fact until later.

And Cases Closed, Inc., was not to take on its third case of murder until later still.

But I am getting ahead of my story.

We left Lincoln at home, under the cool of the willow that hangs over the pond, and Joe and I were on the road at 9:45 precisely. The first of our two barn calls was a progress check on two cases of mastitis at the Crawford Dairy; the second a follow-up on a case of founder at the Swinford Vineyard. I confess to being quite at home in the environs of a professional operation like the Crawford Dairy. Abel Crawford milks more than five hundred cows and ships a little less than three thousand pounds of milk a day. The place is efficiently run, the animals well treated, and the veterinary bill promptly paid. Both human and bovine employees are happy. Madeline says that such farms are my natural milieu.

She is far less sanguine about my attitude toward the ill-equipped hobby farmer. My wife knows me well. In the face of such clients as Jonathan and Penelope Swinford, I tend to lose my aplomb.

I apprised Joe of this as we pulled into the drive leading up to the Swinford barns. "You will discover, my boy, that the amateur farmer can create holy havoc with his animals, with the best of intentions."

Joe looked around and whistled in appreciation. "Some amateur," he said. The winery was one of many such that have sprung up in the Finger Lakes area within the past fifteen years. As the reputation of our grapes spreads worldwide, growers are buying up local farms and transforming them into showplaces like this one. The winery itself sits at the top of a high hill to the right of the house and barn. It resembles an elegant ship, with the prow hanging over the lip of the hill. Visitors to the tasting room have an unparalleled view of the rich valley of grapes below.

On this Saturday morning, the August heat lay like a comforter over the vines, concentrating the sweetness in the fruit. It was a lush and welcome view.

The house was an expensive reproduction of a nineteenth-century Carpenter Gothic. The barn was straight out of the glossier ads in *Equus:* a copper cupola topped the cedar shake roof; the four stalls each debouched to neatly fenced paddocks; flowerbeds alive with marigolds, geraniums, and lavender surrounded the whole.

It was all very pretty.

A brand-new four-horse specialty trailer was parked at the far end of the outdoor arena.

It was all very expensive.

"Oh, the vineyard itself does very well. Swinford knows his grapes. He makes a tolerable red zinfandel and an extremely fine Chardonnay. If his wife and daughter had as much knowledge of horse care as the family does of oenology, we wouldn't be here at all."

Joe flipped through the file. "You and Ally saw the mare Sunny on Monday. Diagnosis was laminitis secondary to overfeeding."

"Correct." I set the emergency brake, got out of the vehicle, and retrieved my case from the trunk. I headed toward the barn.

Joe followed me, still absorbed in the case file.

"You treated the animal with anti-inflammatories. Hey, this is the third visit in six days." He looked up, a slight frown creasing his brow. Joe is tall and skinny. His skinniness is deceptive, as he is quite muscular. "What's going on? It should have resolved itself by now if it was just because the mare got into the feed bin."

"Correct," I said again. We walked to the barn, and I pulled the main door open. A blast of cold air met us. Joe's jaw dropped. "It's air-conditioned?"

I made no response to the obvious. Instead, I called out, "Halloo!" and Penelope Swinford came out of the tack room.

Penelope would benefit from a month or two of Madeline's cooking. She is skinny, and she was dressed in immaculate breeches, paddock boots, and a white sleeveless shirt that smelled faintly of bleach. Her hair was white blonde and roached as short as any filly's for the summer. "Dr. McKenzie!" she said. "I am so glad to see you! Ally's not with you today? She gets on so well with Sunny! But of course, you do, too!" She smiled at Joe. "I take it this is your other assistant?"

Joe reached out and shook her hand

firmly. "Joe Turnblad, Mrs. Swinford."

"Delighted to meet you, Joe." Penelope turned to me. "Ashley's just up at the house. They sent her home from work today, of course. I mean, you heard about the trouble at Tre Sorelle."

I was not interested in any trouble at the dairy. Wherever Doucetta Capretti wielded that goat-headed cane, there was bound to be trouble. "I'd like to see the horse," I said.

"Oh! Sure! Of course! Sunny's not doing too well, I'm afraid. I suppose it's just as well that Ashley's home today so she can talk to you directly. I'll give her a call and get her down here. Come into the tack room for a moment." We followed her into the lavishly appointed room, which I, of course, had seen, and Joe had not. There was a small but well-equipped kitchen. A sectional couch sat in front of wall-to-ceiling windows that looked out over the outdoor arena. The wall opposite the windows was hung with two Steuben saddles, sleek leather bridles, and turnout blankets embroidered with the initials APS.

Penelope buzzed the intercom, chirped brightly into it, then turned to us. "She'll be right down, Dr. McKenzie." She gestured toward the kitchenette. "Can I get you some iced tea? Or coffee?"

All this opulence made me testy. "And the mare?"

"Oh! Of course. Please come this way."

The Swinfords had four horses, an Arab, a Throughbred-Quarterhorse cross with superb hunter conformation, and two Hackney ponies. All were expensive. All were immaculately groomed. All were unexercised, overfed, and had the temperaments of spoiled children.

Sunny was one of the two Hackney ponies. She stood cautiously in the middle of a pile of pristine cedar shavings. I had ordered a strict reduction in feed. Founder is a real danger to a fat horse, and Sunny was still as fat as a Duroc sow. As I approached, she pinned her ears flat against her head, and swung around her hind end. It is the supreme irony of a veterinarian's life that — just like people and dentists — your patients sometimes loathe the sight of you. Sunny was eager to kick me from here to kingdom come.

"Sunny!" Penelope said, as one would to an overindulged baby. "How's my girl today?" She put her hand in her pocket and withdrew a granola bar. "Here's a treat for my girl."

"Stop!" I roared.

Penelope, Joe, and the horse all jerked to

61

attention. I took the granola bar, broke it into pieces, and threw it into a nearby garbage tote. In a considerable state of irritation, I said to Joe, "The twitch, if you please."

Joe removed the twitch from the carryall and followed me into the stall. The twitch is one of the most basic and useful tools available to the veterinarian. Mine is constructed of a length of soft leather — actually, any soft, pliable rope will do — and one pinches it around the animal's upper lip. It operates quite well to get a badly behaved animal's attention. Joe applied the twitch to Sunny's muzzle. He is deft, and he is fast. Sunny didn't have to time to do more than sneeze and give me an evil grin.

I bent to examine the mare's hooves. "Laminitis is an extremely painful condition of the horse hoof, Mrs. Swinford," I said. "The blood pools in the hoof, and there is nowhere for it to go. Imagine, if you will, that you have whacked your thumbnail with a hammer. And then you have to walk on it."

"Oh." Penelope shuddered.

Sunny rolled a cranky eye at me.

"I do see that you have been giving her the bute," I said. "She isn't in pain, although with these feet, she should be. That's good."

I dropped Sunny's left fore and picked up the right. Then I pinched a roll of fat on the mare's barrel. "You have been feeding her grain and hay, have you not? This mare hasn't dropped an ounce since I saw her last." I pulled at my mustache in frustration. "That's very bad. As a matter of fact, it is close to criminal."

Penelope peered at me over the stall door. "But she's starving. Surely just a quart or two of grain can't hurt."

"Absolutely not!" I roared. "You will load this horse up and deliver her to my clinic. Instantly!"

"Yes, Dr. McKenzie."

"And you will not give her one ounce of feed of any kind!"

"Yes, Dr. McKenzie."

I stepped back from the mare and nodded at Joe. He released the twitch. Sunny sneered at me, then nudged at my pockets, presumably looking for sugar. I stepped into the aisle. "You can pick her up in three weeks or so. And I warn you, there is going to be a considerable farrier bill. It's a certain bet that the sole on the left fore has rotated, and the hoof will have to be trimmed and shod with specialty shoes."

"Yes, Dr. McKenzie. Of course, the cost is not a problem. We love Sunny. She was

Ashley's first pony."

"You are loving her to death, madam. If you need help loading the pony up, Joe will give you a hand."

"You mean right now, Dr. McKenzie?"

"If not sooner."

"Hey, Doc. Hey, Ma. What's going on?"

Ashley trotted into the barn like an Afghan hound on parade at Crufts: long, lean, and blonde. She flipped her hair and batted her eyelashes at Joe. "How's Sunny doing?"

"Dr. McKenzie's taking her to the hospital, honey," Penelope said. "The treatment he's been giving her here just doesn't seem to be helping."

I bit my mustache. "It is the treatment you are giving her, madam, that —"

"I don't think I've seen you around before," Joe interrupted. "Ashley, is it?"

"There is a great deal too much of her to see at the moment," I pointed out. The child was dressed — half dressed — in a top that ended far short of her belly button and a pair of shorts not up to the job of covering her buttocks.

Joe put his hand on my shoulder. "Joe Turnblad, Ashley," he said, extending his hand. He shoved me gently aside. It is not at all like the boy to be rude. Perhaps I was being a bit testier than necessary. Madeline occasionally reminds me that human beings deserve the same sort of consideration one gives one's animal patients.

"Hey, Joe," Ashley said. "I *know* I haven't seen you around before." She wriggled in front of her mother. The two of us withdrew to the side, while Joe and Ashley circled around one another. It reminded me of the ritual mating dance of the bowerbird.

"Is Sunny going to be okay, Dr. Mc-Kenzie?" Penelope asked anxiously. "I'd just die if anything happens to her."

I frowned. The woman loved the horse, that was clear. But she had to understand that the animals are not children in horse suits. "Madam," I said. "How would you fare if your routine was to walk twenty miles a day, eating plain, low-protein grass at twenty-minute intervals, drinking five gallons of water a day from untreated streams, sleeping standing up?"

"Me?" She blinked rapidly. "I guess I'd starve to death."

"I guess you would. But that, Penelope, is an ideal life for a horse. Movement. Grass. Fresh air. Water from the stream. You are killing your animals with kindness. Get rid of the air-conditioning! If you must keep the animals in a stall, at least keep a rational amount of manure in the shavings. Not a lot — but a small sufficiency. Keeping the stalls this clean dries out the hoof. Better yet . . ." I threw my arm in a wide circle. "Put the animals outside where they belong! Otherwise your horses will be . . ."

"Deader than a doornail," Ashley said in a thrilling voice. "Honest to God. Right there in the bulk tank."

The mention of a corpse got my attention.

"What did you say, my dear?"

"You haven't heard?" Penelope said. "Oh, my goodness. That poor milk inspector, Melvin somebody . . ."

"Staples," Ashley said. "And oh. My. God. What a hunk. It's a shame, that's what it is. I was, like, totally freaked out."

"Ashley found him stark-staring dead. My poor baby!" Penelope shuddered and drew her daughter close. Ashley shrugged her mother's arm away with an absentminded pat of affection. Clearly, the discovery of Melvin Staples's body, hunk or no, hadn't discomposed her much.

I smoothed my mustache. "How unfortunate for you, my dear. Please tell me what happened."

"It's my summer job. I do, like, data entry for Mrs. Capretti. Anyhow, so I'm sitting at the computer keying in all this crap about pounds of milk per goat and I hear a whack-bang!"

She paused. All eyes were on her.

"It came from the milk room. So I get up and I go over to the door and pull it open a little bit. It's a big, heavy door, you know, so I tug it open a little bit more and I see the door at the other end of the room closing, like."

"Closing like what?" I asked.

Ashley blinked at me. If I hadn't known for a fact she was an honors student in economics at Ithaca College, I would have thought her handicapped. Madeline tells me I have little empathy for the young. "With a bang?" I said impatiently. "Or softly, as if someone were sneaking out?"

"That's a big, heavy door with a counterweight. You can't bang it shut. It closes in its own sweet time."

"I see. And then?"

"And then I go into the room and look around." She mimed tiptoeing about, looking from side to side. "And it was like I was guided. I mean, I just went to the tank and pulled open the lid and there he was. Splooshing around in the milk. We had to dump the whole batch," she added briskly. "Mrs. C. pitched a screaming fit."

"And then what happened?" Joe asked.

67

He was gazing at the girl in fascination.

"Then I went, 'Wow.' And then I went and got Mrs. Capretti and Mrs. Celestine and they called the cops and they sent me home."

"Any indication of the cause of death?" I asked.

Ashley shrugged. "There was a big dent in his head. The milk was pink from the blood. But I suppose they'll have to wait for the autopsy to know for sure."

Law & Order has much to answer for. The young seem to know a great deal about the processes of criminal investigations. "A big dent in his head," I repeated. "Well. It's unlikely that Mr. Staples opened the tank hatch, smacked his head against the rim, and fell into the tank, isn't it?"

"Golly," Penelope said. "Who knew dairies were so dangerous?"

Her daughter looked at her with affectionate contempt. "Gee, Mom. Maybe it was, like, murder. D'ya think?"

"Death of a milk inspector," Joe said. "It sure sounds like murder to me."

We were back at the clinic. The pony Sunny rambled painfully around our indoor arena, which has a soft floor of sand, shavings, and recycled rubber. She would have one thin flake of very dry hay twice a day for the next two weeks and all the water she could drink. I wanted to knock at least one hundred pounds from that pudgy frame. As I had thought, the X-ray of the left fore revealed a slight rotation of the coffin bone, and as soon as the inflammation in the hooves died down, our farrier would begin the slow process of reshaping the hoof. With luck, she'd be sound for light hacking, but only time would tell.

Lincoln was at my side, keeping a sapient eye on the pony's behavior. We have three horses of our own: Ally's Tracker, Andrew, my elderly Quarterhorse, and a Shetland named simply Pony. Horses are herd animals, and they prosper only in the company of others. As Sunny became more comfortable, she would join the others for company. For now, Lincoln himself was on the job. From the way she bared her teeth at the collie, she didn't see it as a privilege.

"Murder, indeed." I turned my attention from the pony's problems to those of the late milk inspector, Melvin Staples. We had done all we could for the pony. Now it was time to do what we could for the deceased.

"He didn't drown without help," a voice behind me said. I turned to see Simon Provost leaning against the arena wall, arms folded across his chest. The Summersville chief of detectives is a man of modest demeanor and a deceptively mild expression. I greeted him with pleasure.

"Simon! I had intended to look you up. And here you are. This is fortuitous."

"You got a minute, Doc?"

"I do," I said cordially. "Shall we repair to the office?"

I had purchased the thirty-acre farm called Sunny Skies some forty years ago, when I had first come to Cornell as an associate professor. The barns, the indoor arena, and the paddocks were the primary attraction. It was only upon my marriage that the house and gardens began to flourish into the comfortable place that they are today, under the attentions of my wife. The outbuildings have always been splendid. The barn has twelve stalls, attached at an L to the large indoor arena. The clinic is housed in the former tack room. It is well, if modestly, equipped. There is a small office, where I receive the occasional client, a room and a toilet in back, where Joe makes his quarters, and a operating-cum-examination room with a clinic chemical analyzer, an X-ray machine, and various other necessities I picked up as Cornell shed equipment outdated for its purposes.

I ushered Simon into the office and sat in the tattered desk chair that has been my companion for almost fifty years. The detective settled into the chair by my desk with a grunt. Joe leaned against the wall. Lincoln nosed the office door open and settled at my feet.

Cases Closed, Inc., had a quorum. We were ready for business.

Provost looked me straight in the eye. "Now, Doc, I don't want you getting any ideas about investigating this murder."

"So it is officially a murder, then?"

"Cause of death hasn't been legally established, no. But he either drowned or died of the blow to the head. We'll know for sure after the coroner's report. Body's off to Syracuse for the forensics."

"I, of course, am not certified to examine the corpses of Homo sapiens, but if you'd like me to take a look on an informal basis . . ."

"No, Doc, I wouldn't. And neither would the State of New York. That half-baked company of yours — what d'ya call it?"

"Cases Closed."

"Right. You have no legal standing. You've got that? You're not even licensed."

I drew breath. Provost held up his hand in admonition. "I don't want to hear it. That honorary deputy certificate I gave you may

71

have been the biggest mistake of my professional life. You aren't a detective, Doc. What you are is a damn good vet, from what I've seen and what everyone tells me. . . ."

"Really?" I said, pleased. "Who is everyone?"

"You know. Everyone. It's a well-known fact."

"My colleagues at Cornell? No? Of course. My newspaper column, Ask Dr. McKenzie!"

Simon rubbed his hands over his face and said, "Argh." Then he said, "What I need from you is veterinary info. And what I'm going to get is veterinary info and *that's as far as it goes!* Got that?"

I smoothed my mustache and smiled.

Simon dug into his jacket pocket for his notebook. In all the time I have known Simon, he has never been without a jacket. He wears a tatterdemalion tweed sports coat in the winter and a crumpled seersucker jacket in the heat. If he wore Birkenstocks, one could mistake him for a professor. "Somatic cell count," he read aloud. "What is it?"

"The number of white blood cells sloughed into a substance such as milk. A high count may be an indicator of an infection such as mastitis. The state sets allowable limits."

"I hear that Tre Sorelle's got some problems in that area. Can the state shut them down? I mean, how big a deal is this milk somatic cell count?"

I tugged at my ear and didn't answer him for a moment. In our past cases, it had sometimes taken Provost a bit more time than necessary to see the desirability of hiring Cases Closed personnel to supplement an investigation. "In cows, it can be a big deal, as you phrase it," I said amiably. "Goats not so much."

"Not so much?"

"Not so much." Years of successfully applying for grants from institutions reluctant to subsidize such vital issues as the constituency of bovine back fat have given me some expertise in the art of negotiation. "I'd be happy to prepare expert testimony that would be well received by the courts."

"But?"

"But it will take some time. Some research."

"And it's gonna cost me."

A small dose of humor was in order. "Madeline would have my guts for garters if it didn't."

Simon's face brightened, his invariable habit when my wife's name is mentioned. "Madeline," he said. "How is she? As a matter of fact, where is she?"

"She went down to the village hall. She intends to have a discussion with the tax inspector."

Simon exhaled sharply. "*That* SOB. Now if someone conked *him* over the head and set him to drown in a bulk tank, you wouldn't hear a shout of surprise from me."

"No?"

"Nossir. You remember Nicky Ferguson retired and took that RV of his to Florida. Well, some dimwit on the village board brought this guy in — his name's Brian Folk, and I don't want to tell you how many 'Folk you' jokes I've been hearing around town." Simon subsided into what in any other person I would have described as a sulk.

"And?" I prompted.

"And he's been a royal pain in the keister. Seems to think it's his God-given duty to raise taxes all over the township. I'm half serious about putting a bodyguard on the guy. Called me twice demanding I do something about these threats he's been getting. Told him not much I could do unless he was actually attacked. And it's not going to be long before that happens." He rubbed his face again. "So Maddy's down at the town hall giving him what for, huh? Well.

Fine. If anyone can take that miserable little punk down a peg, it's your wife. She's something else, Austin."

"She is, indeed," I said proudly. "As to our murder victim, Simon . . ."

"He's not 'our' anything, Doc. We're hiring you on as a goat consultant so I can figure out if anyone at the dairy had a motive to knock him off."

"At the usual rates?" I asked.

"Sure. Whatever. The usual rates."

"Excellent. Now, what do you know of this man's background?"

Simon eyed me suspiciously.

"I need to know only in support of my report. If the man had little or no expertise in the area of somatic cell testing, that could affect the results."

"Of course he knew what he was doing. He was licensed by the State of New York."

He bit his lip. I did not comment.

"You may have a point. I'll see what I can come up with for you." Simon paged through his book. "We tossed his name into the computer, of course, and we haven't got any bites yet."

"By which you mean he has no arrest record."

"Nope. Seems to have been an okay kind of guy, from the first accounts. He's a vet.

Not like you, but a veteran. Spent more time than he should have in the first Gulf War but then all our people over there have spent more time than they should. Honorable discharge, according to his wife."

I remembered young Ashley's appraisal of the dead man's appearance. A hunk, she'd said. "He was married?"

"Tough little thing. Name's Kelly. All cut up about this, of course. Two kids. Anyhow, she says Staples grew up near Seneca Falls, went from high school right into the marines, and then qualified as a milk inspector two years ago."

"He must have grown up on a farm," I observed. "The state does require two years of significant agricultural experience."

Simon tucked the notebook into his pocket. "So that's what I know about the deceased. Seems to have been a decent enough guy, although you never know, these days." He leaned forward, his elbows on his knees. "I was thinking maybe there was some way you could get into that dairy. Sniff around there. From what I can tell, there's been trouble with this . . ."

"MSCC," Joe said. "The milk somatic cell count."

"That. I need to know if anyone at the dairy had a viable motive to off this guy."

"You've talked to Doucetta Capretti?" Provost groaned. "That I have, Doc. And here's what I figure. Better you than me!"

THREE

My decision to forgo supervising the Tre Sorelle QMPS team had been precipitate; I needed legitimate access to the dairy if Cases Closed were to solve the murder.

Doucetta Capretti had a short fuse. I doubted she would answer questions voluntarily if I presented myself as a detective. As a QMPS consultant, I would have more standing in her eyes. I tried not to think of the fate of a former colleague, who had been rapped smartly on the backside when he questioned Doucetta's brining practices at a meeting of the New York State Farmstead and Artisan Cheese Makers Guild.

A phone call to Neville Brandstetter's office informed me that I would find him at home. I sent Joe to the Internet to research New York state requirements for safe somatic cell levels in goat milk and any scientific papers on the causes of increased levels.

The GPS in the Bronco directed me to the south side of Summersville where the Brandstetters made their home. He had been married to the volatile Anna Luisa for twenty years. There was much I could learn from Neville about the dairy where his wife had spent her girlhood. I hoped he was in a forthcoming mood.

When I stopped in front of his house, I began to have doubts about his cheeriness of mind. Brandstetter was a precise and tidy man with a lively interest in horticulture. But the lawn and gardens around his house were in a pitiable state. The lawn was in need of mowing. The perennial bed cried out for weeding.

A colleague of mine once said that one could hazard a guess on the state of a couple's marriage by the state of the landscaping. If so, the Brandstetters' union was not a happy one.

The house was in the Craftsman style, an architectural mode common to this part of New York. It sat attractively in the middle of a sizable lot. The shingled roof hung low over the front porch, which had a deserted air. A fawn beagle lay on the front stoop, with its head on its paws. It raised its head when Lincoln barked as I parked in the short driveway, and then trundled down the steps to greet us, tail slowly wagging. It was a bitch, and a nice one. Her coat was glossy and she was not fat, as is often the case when this breed has been turned into a pet. (The proper role of a beagle is beagling, not playing fetch with indolent owners.) She greeted Linc with a submissive wriggle and thrust her head under my hand for a pat. The front door opened and Brandstetter stepped out onto the porch.

"McKenzie," he said. "Haven't seen you in some time. You're looking well."

I couldn't say the same of Brandstetter. His red beard was a veritable hedge. There were purple shadows under his eyes. His skin was sallow. If he had been a cow, I'd have tested him for Johne's disease. He bent and ruffled Lincoln's ears. "And how are you, Linc?" He straightened up with a sigh. "Bergland told you about the dairy job, I suppose. I take it you've heard?"

"About the death of the milk inspector? Yes, I have."

He grinned. It was not a happy expression. More of a grimace. "They've closed the dairy temporarily, but from what I hear they'll be up and running pretty quick. You can imagine Doucetta's reaction to dumping all that milk."

I could, indeed. The laws of man can shut

down machinery, but they can't stop a goat from lactating.

"She's been on the phone to the governor by now, I imagine," he added gloomily.

"Had you met the deceased?"

"Staples?" There was that strange grin again. I wondered if the man was about to colic. "Sure. The goat industry's growing, Austin. We're getting new cheese makers and new milk producers all the time. Most of 'em have some start-up problems of one sort or another. So Staples called me for advice once or twice. Seemed to know his job." He flushed red, then white.

"I would be quite interested in supervising the QMPS team at Tre Sorelle," I said. "Victor may have mistaken my intent when I spoke with him yesterday."

"Eh?"

"You haven't spoken to Victor since he's spoken to me?"

"I? No. I haven't checked my phone messages today. I've been feeling a bit under the weather."

"You look like hell," I said frankly.

"Do I?" He tugged at his beard with an absentminded air. He turned to go back to the house. I followed. "Some kind of summer flu, I think. Came on all of a sudden. Late yesterday."

I was close enough to smell the alcohol on the man's breath. Summer flu, my hat. There was a mystery here, for certain. If Brandstetter had taken to the bottle, Victor would have been the first to tell me.

"So I went home from the office yesterday and . . ." He trailed off. "Won't you come in? Can I get you something?" He pushed open the door. "Scotch?"

"A bit early in the day for me, thank you all the same."

Lincoln followed me in. The little beagle followed Linc. The living room wasn't too much of a tip. From Brandstetter's personal disarray, I'd expected worse. Several days' worth of the *New York Times* were spread over the floor, and the remains of the man's lunch occupied the coffee table in front of the fireplace. I settled into the leather armchair at right angles to the couch. Linc sat at my knee. The beagle nestled adoringly at Lincoln's side. He licked her nose, and then turned his attention to the business at hand.

"I'll check and see if Victor called, shall I?" Brandstetter wandered over to the telephone stand in the corner and punched a button on the answering machine. The first voice I recognized was that of his wife, Anna Luisa. It was high and hysterical and the only thing I heard before Neville slammed his hand on the machine to shut it off was: "Neville? Oh, God!"

"Not trouble, I hope?"

Neville wandered back to the couch in a distracted way. He ran his hands through his beard. "No, no. She called me at the office. Thought she'd find me here first, I guess. I took care of it. Just a . . ." He paused. "Flat tire."

The Caprettis were known for volatility, but I doubted a flat tire would have engendered that kind of response. Didn't the woman have AAA? I waited with an expectant air, but Neville merely continued his aimless wandering about the room. There is nothing like a work-related problem to take a man's mind off his personal woes, so I said:

"What's your take on the somatic cell count problem at the dairy?"

I only half listened to Brandstetter's response. I knew the gist anyway, and I was trying to read the heading on a pile of papers half covered by an abandoned salami sandwich. One can't help being familiar with judicial actions in these litigious times, and it looked remarkably like a summons and complaint. The summoned was Neville; the plaintiff Anna Luisa Capretti Brandstetter and the cause of action was a divorce.

"Oh, dear," I said.

"It *is* a bit of a mystery," Neville said with some animation. "Doucetta runs a tight ship. And of course, goats are prone to higher somatic cell counts than other ruminants. It's not a reliable indicator at all. A cell count of over a million in bovines is a sure sign of mastitis or worse."

"Not necessarily," I said. It was, in fact, a gross calumny, but the man had not spent fifty years studying cows. "There can be a number of contributing factors."

"Yes, well, you're the cow man. Anyway, goat counts go up if the doe is at the end of lactation, or if she's a big producer, or even if it's spring." The problem at hand had indeed served to distract him from whatever personal woe was bothering him. He leaned forward, interest in his eyes. "Leslie Chou's right. There is quite a nice little problem here. Why are the counts so high? And why so consistently?"

"Stress?" I suggested. "Are the animals confined twenty-four hours a day?"

"The goats are pastured. This time of year, they only come in for milking. The less stress on the animal, the better a producer it'll be. Doucetta learned that early on."

"Then a contaminant in the pasture?"

Goats, like all farm animals, are vulnerable to toxic weeds and grasses.

"Odd time of year for it. But it's certainly possible. Yes, it's quite a nice little problem."

"Do you think Doucetta herself has any ideas about the source?"

"She ought to — but good luck in getting it out of her. You know what she's like. On the other hand, that dairy is her life. She'd probably set aside her temper if you were going to help her out of a jam," Neville said as if trying to convince himself. "I know she thumped Abrahamson with that damn cane of hers when he went in to talk to her about the feta, but that was different. More personal. She takes a lot of pride in her cheese."

I'd forgotten about Abrahamson. "Broke his shin, didn't she?"

"Well, he had a pretty good bruise, that's for sure. But I kind of admire the old girl. For heaven's sake, Austin. She admits to ninety-four but I wouldn't be surprised if she's closer to a hundred. And she's got all her marbles." He gave me a genuine smile, which lightened the care lines in his face. "And some of mine."

"Hm. So the key to getting along with her would be?"

"Getting along?" Neville laughed. "With

Doucetta? Nobody gets along with Doucetta. The trick is to avoid World War Three." He shrugged. "Just agree with everything she says. That should do it." His eyes slid toward the salami sandwich and the horrible document that lay beneath. "Luisa just never figured that out."

I cleared my throat. A detective must go where sensible men fear to tread. "And how is Anna Luisa? The last time we saw her was at my retirement party, I believe."

Neville's lip quivered. He bit his lip. He began to cry.

It was most awkward. Tears rolled down his face into his beard. His nose ran. I got up, prepared to leave the man alone with his sorrow. I do not, as Madeline would have it, panic in the face of emotion. But I admit my attention was on leaving the man to his sorrow with a reasonable grace.

Had I been paying attention to my dog instead of Brandstetter's dripping nose, Anna Luisa's entrance into the house would not have taken me by surprise. Lincoln looked toward the front door. His ears tuliped forward. He rose, wagging his tail. The little beagle jumped to her feet, too, eyes adoringly on Linc's face. Anna Luisa burst into the room with a rush of air. She carried a suitcase and a tote bag stuffed with clothes.

The look on Neville's face when he saw her was very like the beagle's.

Doucetta's daughters are quite good-looking, with black curly hair, eyelashes as long as a Guernsey heifer's, and curvy figures. Luisa is perhaps the prettier of the two, although at the moment she looked quite upset. Her face was flushed and tears streaked her cheeks. Between Neville's tears and runny nose, the two of them made a fairly soggy pair. She set the suitcase and the tote bag on the floor, flung herself at Neville's feet, and cried, "Darling. Forgive me!"

A detective cannot afford sensitivity. I quelled my impulse to run for it. It is a drawback to the occupation I had not heretofore encountered. If I left this poignant scene, I might never discover the reason why Luisa had left in the first place, much less why she had returned. All facts are fodder in an investigation. I sat back in my chair and prepared to listen.

Neville pulled a handkerchief from his pocket and blew his nose. "Forget it."

"I came back because I love you! Not him!"

Aha. A lover, then. A sad story, but all too common.

There was only one fact I needed to know, and then I could leave them to their discussion. I cleared my throat to capture their attention. "And who is the gentleman in the case?"

Before either Brandstetter could respond, my cell phone rang. It was Deirdre, the barmaid at the Embassy. There was trouble involving my wife, the tax assessor, and the remains of a lemon pie.

I was out of the house in a flash.

"Oh, Lordy," Madeline said. "You actually asked poor Neville Brandstetter who tried to run off with his wife?"

I poked at my salad greens with my fork. I had paid Deirdre for the lemon pie and it was time for lunch. By the time Lincoln and I arrived at the Embassy, Brian Folk had stalked off to wash up, and my wife was fomenting revolution among the remaining patrons. She greeted me with pleasure and a tuna salad.

"There was no need to come and rescue me, darlin'," she added before I could respond to her question about the Brandstetters' troubles. "I had everything well in hand."

"I believe it was the pie in hand that caused the trouble," I said.

"Ha-ha," Madeline said flatly. "That little skunk."

"Neville? I believe Neville to be the innocent party in this case."

"Not Neville. That Brian person. Do you know he went and upped taxes in the trailer park down by Covert?" She nodded toward the bar, where two large, husky fellows in John Deere billed hats were drowning their tax sorrows in Rolling Rock. "Those poor souls barely have two nickels to rub together as it is. And how in holy heck is a flippin' trailer supposed to appreciate, anyway? Those things lose half their value the minute some poor sucker drives one off the lot." Indignation made her cheeks pink. It was quite becoming.

"I know very little about trailer parks," I admitted. "I could hazard a guess, however, that the application of the lemon pie did little for our chances at a reduction in fees."

"The archangel Gabriel himself couldn't get that little bum to roll his assessment back," Madeline said matter-of-factly. "The man's a pinhead and a bozo. If I were back in Memphis, I'd make a few calls about tar and feathers."

I looked at her in some alarm. She patted my hand reassuringly, sighed, and took a large bite of the Monrovian Special.

(Madeline does not have a problem with cholesterol.) "I did find something else out, though," she said through the hamburger. "He has it in for Tre Sorelle, too."

"Oh?"

" 'Look, fatty!' he said to me, in this snippy way. 'That old bat Capretti didn't get anywhere with me and neither will you.' "

"I beg your pardon? He called you *what?*"

Madeline patted my hand again. "Don't fuss, darlin'. That's when I grabbed the pie and clocked him with it."

"It was your magnificent figure, my dear, that first attracted me to you," I said with some emotion. "I have told you, often, that you remind me of those great beauties of the past. Lillie Langtry, for example."

"Thank you, Austin." She finished the hamburger with a sigh and toyed idly with an onion ring. "Anyway, short of getting the crumb a job somewhere else — like Siberia — we seem to be stuck with him for the moment. But it's interesting, don't you think? That he had this go-round with Doucetta the very day the milk inspector ends up in the bulk tank? I hear she took a swing at him with that cane of hers. Brian Folk, not Melvin Staples. Maybe she missed and got Staples by mistake."

I ignored this little joke. "At the moment, we have bits and pieces of seemingly unrelated information. The Brandstetters' fractured marriage. The confrontation between Doucetta and the tax inspector. The mysteriously high somatic cell counts. As you know, it is a tenet of Cases Closed that random facts in a case do come together to form a pattern. A murder investigation is much like diagnosing an underlying pathology in a cow or a horse. One observes and assesses the overt symptoms. . . ."

"Oh, glory," Madeline said. "There's Simon. And look who's with him."

We were in our usual booth, which is halfway down the length of the restaurant, and I was on the side that faced the Gents. I turned around, the better to see the front door. Simon had entered and was in quiet colloquy with Deirdre at the bar. She gestured toward us. Simon raised his hand in greeting, nodded to Deirdre, and headed our way. She then turned to the phone behind the bar and picked up the receiver.

I was usually glad to see Simon. My pleasure was considerably tempered by the fact that he was accompanied by a short, ferret-faced fellow who looked weaselly enough to be a tax assessor. My guess was buttressed by the fact that a dollop of lemon pie adhered to his shirt collar. I raised my eyebrows and looked at Madeline.

"Yep," she said cheekily.

"Perhaps Simon has obtained the autopsy results and is bringing them over to us and he fell in with Folk on the way," I said. "I don't know how you feel about it, my dear, but I find the forensics to be absolutely essential to the intelligent progress of a case."

"It's way too soon to have any forensic results. And what would Brian Folk be doin' with him if he did? Nope." She smiled. "Simon's come to arrest me."

Simon looked rather grim. Brian Folk looked smug. Simon sat down next to me and addressed my wife. "Mrs. McKenzie. Maddy. Did you assault Brian Folk with a pie?" Brian Folk leaned against a nearby booth, his arms folded across his chest.

"You bet I did."

"She admits it!" Brian Folk said with a vicious smirk. "In front of witnesses, too."

Simon leaned down and banged his forehead gently against the table.

"I wish," Madeline added sunnily, "that it had been a larger pie. It was more of a tart, really."

Simon rolled his eyes upward, and then sat back. "He wants to press charges. He wants me to arrest you for battery."

"Maddy!"

All three of us turned to the front door. That shriek was familiar. It belonged to Rita Santelli, my editor and the publisher of the *Summersville Sentinel.* Rita is a thin, peppery widow in her midforties. She has a great many freckles, shrewd gray eyes, and short brown hair streaked prematurely gray. She sat down next to Maddy in a flurry, tape recorder at the ready, a camera jouncing against her meager bosom. "I just heard. Did you whack that damn fool tax inspector with a lemon pie?" She rolled her head, looked at Folk, and gave an artificial start of surprise. "Oh! Why there you are, Inspector. Sorry. I didn't see you standing there."

"That's libel, that is," Brian Folk said. "Calling me a damn fool."

"It would be slander if anything," I said. "And it isn't."

Rita's eyes flickered toward Simon and back again. "I was hoping I could get a picture of you with one of Charley's pies, Maddy? Sort of held over your head? And if bozo here wants to be in the picture, so much the better."

"It was more of a tart, really," Madeline said. "But you bet I will."

Rita huddled forward and lowered her voice. Brian Folk leaned over my shoulder the better to hear. His breath smelled of cheese. "The thing is, I'm in the middle of an article about the tax assessor's egregious abuse of power in small towns like Summersville and I figure the photo will be a great illustration."

"Illustrating what?" Simon said. "Rule by pie?"

"Very funny. No, it'll illustrate the first step in a taxpayer's revolution!" Rita leaned back. "I figure this kind of news is just what the public wants to hear, especially in an election year." She dug into her skirt pocket, pulled out her cell phone, and waved it over her head. "I'm about to call Gordy Rassmussen. You all know Gordy, right? Been town supervisor for years. And the guy that hired *you,* right?" She glared at Folk. "And seeing how it *is* an election year, and how Gordy just loves all the media exposure he can get . . ."

Gordy, a Swede, was notoriously camera shy.

". . . He's going to love justifying the rise in taxes in this town. And then" — she gave Folk a sinister smile — "I'm going to go into a lot of depth about a tax assessor's qualifications. Did you know that you don't have to have any kind of special training to be a tax assessor? That it's — hmmm, what's the word I want — patronage, that's it. That it's a patronage sort of job. I think you could even call it sort of a payoff, under certain circumstances."

"This is blackmail," Brian Folk said hoarsely.

"This is nothing of the kind," Rita snapped. "This is American journalism at its finest. Why, I bet I could even get some of the city news teams out to cover this. We could open the news show with video interviews of some of the poor souls whose taxes have priced them right out of their homes, kind of like those fellows over there." She raised her hand and hollered, "Whooee, Deirdre! Whyn't you bring Spike and Killer over for a little talk about their taxes?"

Deirdre shepherded the two gentlemen at the bar toward our booth. Both were substantially built. One of them nodded graciously at Madeline. The other made a fist of his right hand and smacked it into the palm of his left. Brian Folk stiffened, made a noise between a gargle and a snort, and headed toward the door. He opened it, turned, and sent a chilling glance our way.

The door closed behind him, to a momentary silence.

"Ha," Deirdre said, "That'll teach the

little piker to stiff *me* on a tip. Lester? Darryl? I got a beer at the bar for you boys. And Maddy? Any time you want to smack that guy in the snoot, there's another couple of pies in the back."

She marched back to the bar, a victorious swing to her hips.

"Pretty good move, there, Rita," Simon said. "Unless you're really planning on running a couple of stories about this?"

Rita set the recorder down on the table. "Deirdre called and said Maddy'd end up in the joint if I didn't get down here quick. Not," she admitted, "that I wouldn't have had a pretty good story if he hadn't backed off. Anyhow, I didn't do all that much." She grinned at us. "Me, I think it was Lester and Darryl that convinced our Mr. Folk to sulk in silence. Spike and Killer, hah! That was a pretty good one."

"Do you think it was the threat of violence that drove him off?" I asked thoughtfully. "I observed him rather closely during this entire altercation. I don't believe it was the prospect of one in the snoot that dissuaded him from persecuting my wife. It was something you said, Rita."

"About the power of the press, you mean?" Rita said with a pleased air.

"No. About his qualifications. He jumped,

as if startled. The pupils of his eyes widened. His autonomic nervous system betrayed him."

"His what?" Simon asked irritably.

"He exhibited the classic signs of guilt."

The silence at the table was, I believe, quite respectful.

"McKenzie," Provost said. "That's the biggest bunch of hooey I've ever heard. With all due respect."

"No, no," Rita said excitedly. "The CIA uses that kind of technique all the time. I've read about it. Even the smoothest of liars can't control unconscious reactions. You really think if I dig around we can get something on this guy?" Her eyes were sparkling with excitement.

"I can only go as far as I have. But if you were to ask me to bet on it, I would. The man has something to hide."

Rita rubbed her hands together in glee. "Oh, that'd be one heck of a story. Now." She fixed her gaze on the lieutenant and poised her finger over the tape recorder. "About the current top story of the week. What's going on with this murder?"

Provost shook his head. "Darn shame, isn't it? Losing the milk inspector like that."

"That's the official quote from the police department?"

"We're pursuing our inquiries."

"Been reading English mystery novels in your spare time, have you?" Rita said. "C'mon, Lieutenant. Nigel's out at the dairy interviewing Mrs. Capretti. You're going to want a chance to tell your side of the story."

Nigel Fish is Rita's chief (and, truth be told, only) investigative reporter. Aside from a slipshod approach to the finer points of the English language, he is probably a pretty good one. His chief flaw is a romantic crush on Allegra, which she handles with aplomb, when not frankly annoyed.

"Now, Rita. I wouldn't say the police department had one side of the story and Mrs. Capretti, bless her soul, the other." Rather absentmindedly, he took a sip of my coffee. I have mentioned that Provost's mild manner and bland demeanor are misleading. Behind that slightly dopey expression, I could see that his mind was working furiously.

"Well?" With a poke of her forefinger, Rita turned the recorder on.

"Melvin Staples was a valued member of the Summersville community. His loss will be felt in many quarters."

Rita poked the tape recorder off. "Phooey. What's with the smarmy political blabber?

Did somebody die and leave you mayor? Mel Staples was a good-looking hunk who diddled half the eligible ladies in 'the Summersville community.' I want to know how he died and whether you have any suspects. That wife of his, for example. She was a discus thrower in high school. She could have clocked him over the head and stuffed him into the bulk tank dead easy. Or any number of pissed-off husbands."

Angry husbands? "Good heavens," I said. "Neville Brandstetter."

Rita turned the recorder back on.

I turned to Provost. "I thought you said she was all cut up about his death," I said. "Mrs. Staples, that is."

Provost looked reprovingly at me. "The investigation's only a few hours old."

"So *that's* how you want me to quote you in the paper? The investigation's only a few hours old?"

"The body of Melvin Staples, milk inspector for the State of New York agricultural department, was discovered at approximately nine thirty this morning in the bulk tank located at the Tre Sorelle Dairy off Route 96. The cause of death has not been determined. The Summersville Police Department's working on the case and expects to have further information shortly." Provost drained the rest of my coffee and stood up. "As soon as I have any more information, Rita, I'll let you know. In the meantime, if you'll excuse me, I have suspects to interview." He hitched his trousers up and marched toward the door.

Rita watched him leave with a ruminative expression. She then turned to me. "So, Austin. What's the real deal, here? Are you and that business of yours, what's it called, Cases Closed, that's right. Are you in on this case?"

"No comment," I said, rather proudly.

Rita's eyes lit up. "So you *are* on the case? Who's this Neville Bran-whatsis? Have you been out to the dairy? Do you have any suspects yet?"

"Who said anything about Neville Brandstetter?"

"You did," Rita said. "When I told you about Staples and the pissed-off husbands. Brandstetter. With two *t*'s?"

"I doubt that Neville has anything to do with this," I said. "And as for the activities of Cases Closed, we will apprise you when appropriate."

Rita sighed, turned the tape recorder off, and stuffed it into her tote. "I'd better get to the paper. Nigel'll be calling in his story pretty soon." She reached over and gave

Madeline a hug. "It's a shame when the wrong people get clocked, isn't it, Maddy? Now if someone were to smack that Brian Folk, we'd run a nice big headline along the lines of 'Ding Dong, the Witch Is Dead.' Or 'Warlock' as the case may be." She scowled. "Do you know what my tax bill on my building's going to be this year?"

"He's upped the appraisal on the news-paper building, too?" Madeline said. "Lordy. That man is cruisin' for a bruisin'."

"Make me up a couple of pies and send them on over. We can bombard him to-gether. Gotta go! Bye!" Rita gathered up her various accoutrements and headed out.

"It wasn't really a pie," Madeline said after her retreating figure. "More of a tart."

FOUR

"I didn't have anywhere near the interesting day you guys did," Allegra complained. "I didn't get the chance to hit anybody with a pie. All I did was practice half passes with Tracker."

"It was most satisfyin'," Madeline admitted. "But it wasn't all that big a pie."

We were gathered for an early dinner. Allegra had a date with some friends to attend a concert in Ithaca. Joe had a Saturday night stint behind the bar at the Embassy. This left us little time for a preliminary meeting on the case I had designated the Ill-Gotten Goat, primarily because I feared Staples was dead because he had gotten the goat of a jealous husband.

Madeline set a bowl of fruit salad on the table. Joe poured iced tea. We all settled at our places. I passed the plate of baked chicken to Joe and helped myself to mashed potatoes.

"And as for poor Dr. Brandstetter" — Allegra turned her big green eyes on me — "did you really ask him who tried to run off with Mrs. Brandstetter?"

"I did."

Joe plucked two rolls out of the bread basket and covered them with butter. Madeline handed me a roll — they were still warm from the oven — but removed the butter to a prudent distance. "So did you find out who the guilty guy was?" he asked.

"I did not." I did not voice my suspicions.

"It's a terrible thing, messin' around," Madeline said with a sigh. "I mean, look at poor old Victor. If he hadn't had that little friskiness with that youngster from his small ruminants class, he'd be a happier man right now. What that woman needs," she added, "is something to take her mind off of all that money."

"You mean Mrs. Bergland? Or Mrs. Brandstetter?" Ally asked. "Mrs. Brandstetter has a lot of money. You know she wears a chinchilla coat in the wintertime? Fur! Can you believe it?"

"Both of them, I suppose. Anna Luisa's always been at loose ends. She never liked the dairy work. I think she trained as a teacher in a high school, but she gave that up when the schools started laying off teachers because of the budget cuts. And they never had any kids. But I was talking about Thelma. She just plain needs something to keep her busy old body occupied."

"Like what?" Ally asked.

"*I* was thinking maybe . . . cheese making."

The three of us stared at her.

"Cheese making?" I said.

"I signed the two of us up for the cheese-making class at Tre Sorelle today."

Long familiarity with my wife's thought processes led me to the proper conclusion. "My dear — that's brilliant."

Madeline twinkled at me. "It's a three-day course. It starts Tuesday. There were two spaces left in the class. I figure we can pick up any number of clues to help the investigation along."

"Are we pretty sure the murderer's at the dairy, though?" Ally asked.

"We can be sure that the murderer made at least one appearance at the dairy," Joe said with a tinge of sarcasm.

Allegra shot him a look. The two had been rivals ever since the competition for the job as clinic assistant. There was détente, with occasional flare-ups. Odie tolerated Lincoln in much the same way.

"Excellent question, Ally. Staples seems to

have had a talent for annoying a significant part of the village population. Therefore," I continued, "we must look into Staples's background as well as the Caprettis and their relations. For all we know, Staples may have been followed to the dairy by a total outsider. The murderer may have followed him into the milk room and simply took advantage of an opportunity to hit him over the head and push him in. There are a number of possible suspects. I have, therefore, made a plan." I reached over to the bookshelf that divides our kitchen from the dining area and picked up the folder I'd started. It was labeled CC005.

"Really?" Ally said. "I've made a plan, too."

Joe reached into the pocket of his T-shirt and waved a folded piece of paper in the air. "And me."

"Well, isn't that nice," Madeline said comfortably. "We can put them all together. My plan's just to go to those cheese classes and collect all the scuttlebutt floating around."

"My plan's to suck up to Ashley," Ally said. "She's taking some second-level dressage from Mrs. Gernsback. I'm going to take Tracker over there and show up for the Tuesday afternoon class. She's been at the data entry job all summer, right? I'll bet she knows stuff about the dairy she doesn't even know she knows."

"And Joe and I will be on the QMPS team in the guise of consultants," I said. "I plan to meet with young Leslie Chou on Monday morning and arrive at the dairy Monday afternoon.

"There are certain facts we need to establish to obtain a clear picture of what occurred that morning. If you all would take notes, please, we will list the basics."

There was a brief flurry of activity as the others assembled a pen and pad (Madeline) and iPhones (Ally and Joe).

"We will make an assumption that the relevant times are between nine thirty a.m. on Saturday, when the morning's milking was finished, and eleven a.m., when the body was discovered. We need to know who was at the dairy and where they were during those hours. We will check with the milk board and Melvin's wife to determine his activities prior to his appearance in the bulk tank." I looked over the rim of my spectacles at them. "We must keep our minds open to any and all possibilities. At the moment, we don't even have a viable list of suspects."

"Do we have any sort of forensics?" Joe asked.

I frowned. Provost had exhibited his usual recalcitrance when I requested the scene-of-the-crime data and the autopsy report. His response, in fact, had been to stick with the goats. "Not yet," I admitted.

Lincoln, who had been dozing in his basket by the woodstove, suddenly leaped to his feet and padded to the back door. A frantic tattoo of rapping made him bark.

"Somebody's here," Ally said.

"Perhaps it's Ashley come to visit Sunny," Madeline said. "How's the pony doin'?"

"As well as can be expected," I said. "If she has come to give the animal food, we will bar the door."

The rapping increased in intensity. Joe shoved his chair back. Before he got to his feet, the door burst open and Anna Luisa Brandstetter tumbled into the kitchen. Her black hair tumbled wildly around her face. The sclera around her pupils was visible. She panted heavily. I quelled an impulse to reach for a dose of acepromazine.

"Dr. McKenzie! You've got to help me! They've arrested Neville for murder!"

"I don't know what rotten gossip went blabbing to the police about Mel," Anna Luisa said furiously, after Madeline had calmed her down, "but I'd like to kill her myself."

I cleared my throat and offered a second stiff brandy to Neville's distraught wife. She downed it on one gulp and ranted on. "And I don't know why they dragged Neville off to jail or what evidence they think they have, but this is just terrible."

As soon as we had ascertained that Luisa had no physical trauma, Joe and Allegra had exchanged one significant glance and exited the house, leaving Luisa in Madeline's capable hands. Luisa's hysteria had rapidly transmuted into a temper tantrum. I hoped sufficient brandy would tamp the rage into a manageable blaze. I poured a third tot and offered it to her.

"Oh. Why! *Why! Why!*" she shrieked. She threw herself facedown on our leather sectional sofa and beat her hands against the cushions.

Madeline caught my concerned gaze and shrugged. "It's leather, sweetie. It can take it." And then, rather sharply, "That's enough, Luisa, dear. If you can sit up and let us know exactly what happened, Austin and I may be able to help you. Here." She removed the brandy from my grasp and handed it to Luisa. "Third time's the charm."

Luisa took the glass, held it in both hands, much as a toddler would, and gulped it down. She looked up at us with that same, toddlerlike expression. "I'm so frightened," she whispered. "What if they hang poor Neville?"

"Nonsense," I said. "They haven't hanged felons in New York state for years. He'd die by lethal injection, if anything."

"Um, Austin?" Madeline said.

"Eh? Oh. Of course it won't come to that, Luisa. Unless he did it." I paused. "Did he?"

"I'm so afraid he did," she whispered. "I'm so afraid he did!" She began to wind up like the fire horn at the village fire department.

"Anna Luisa," Madeline said briskly. "You're fifty-two years old and you are made of sterner stuff than this. Now sit up and tell us exactly what happened."

Luisa scowled, perhaps at the mention of her age, and sat up as instructed.

"Please begin at the beginning, go on, and then stop," I said.

"It was that wretched little witch. Mel's wife. That police lieutenant went back to her house and asked her point-blank if Mel and I had been having an affair and she, do you know what? She had pictures!"

"Good heavens," I said. "Do you know how they were obtained?"

"She claims she got them through the

mail." Luisa shrugged. "She's lying. Of course. She got somebody to follow us. Or maybe she was the one who followed us."

"Did Neville get similar pictures?"

"He didn't know a thing about Mel! Not until that police lieutenant marched into my house and dragged him off to jail!"

"But clearly Neville knew you were having an affair with someone," I suggested gently.

"Well, yes." Luisa looked thoughtful. "Maybe — hm. You may as well know it all."

It was an old story, and a familiar one. The lovers had met at the dairy. Sparks flew. They decided to run away together. Et cetera, et cetera, et cetera. Whoever said Tolstoy was wrong about happy families being all alike — that it was unhappy families who are all alike — got it in one. I cut short the banal recounting of the progress of the affair and asked Luisa about the day before the murder.

"I called Neville at the office and told him I was leaving. That I'd found someone else. That the lawyers would be in touch."

"Just like that?" Madeline asked. "I mean, you didn't try to soften it any?"

"Soften it?" Luisa blinked at her. "Well, it was true, and Neville deserved the truth, didn't he?"

Madeline sighed a little. Then she said, "Please go on."

The eloping couple spent the night at an apartment Luisa had rented in Ithaca. Mel left for work the next day. He'd intended to come home for lunch. He didn't arrive. Luisa heard the news of his death on the radio.

"And then I called Neville. I mean, I couldn't think of anything else to do. I left a message for him. He was at the office. Or in the field. Or teaching. Anywhere," she said bitterly, "except there for me. And I sat there in that apartment for a couple of hours. Then I went home. Everything," she added even more bitterly, "was all patched up until that lieutenant showed up."

"Is there any actual evidence involving Neville in Staples's murder?" I asked.

Luisa shrugged.

"Did Simon actually arrest him? Or just take him in for questioning?"

"Simon?"

" 'That lieutenant,' " Madeline said rather dryly.

"Oh. I don't know." Her bosom began an ominous heaving. Tears welled up in her eyes. "I was just so upset I couldn't stop screaming."

"Quick, Austin, the brandy!"

We gave Luisa a fourth tot, which seemed

to stave off the hysterics for the moment.

"It's possible that Neville hasn't been arrested at all, but has just been taken down to the village station for questioning," I said. "If you couldn't stop screaming it's unlikely that either man was able to hear himself think."

"Is it possible?" Luisa cried, clasping her hands in that childlike way. "Do you think they'll let him go?"

"I'll call and find out," Madeline said kindly. She withdrew to the kitchen, where she could call the station in relative quiet.

"Tell me about the dairy," I suggested. "Is there anyone there who might have a reason to, ah . . ."

"Kill Mel?" Luisa shook her head. "Only Neville." She paused reflectively. "He's crazy about me, Neville is. I'm afraid it's all too possible that he did discover who I'd fallen in love with. And then . . . yes, he had motive to do it. He was insanely jealous. Oh. Oh, this is all so sad! I just couldn't help it, Austin. It's just the way I am. I've got to be loved! I've got to!"

"Neville's on his way home right now," Madeline said briskly, coming back into the living room.

"Do you think . . . that is . . . has he forgiven me?"

"I have no idea," Madeline said. "Are you feelin' fit enough to drive, sweetie? Would you like me to take you back? Austin can follow us in your car."

"*No!* No! I can't stay the night with a murderer! Can't I stay here? I feel safe here!"

I could not suppress a shudder. What if my tenderhearted wife agreed to let this poor benighted harpy stay in the back room?

"Lieutenant Provost says that your husband's in the clear."

"Is he *sure?*" Luisa said skeptically. "Neville's quite clever, you know."

"He was teaching a summer school class from nine to eleven this morning."

"Parasitology," Luisa said. "Yes. It's a graduate course." She looked thoughtful. "I forgot all about that."

"Those hours cover the possible time of death." Madeline folded her lips, which made the dimples on either cheek stand out. "So you won't be spending the night with a murderer." She held a hand out to Luisa. "Come on, sweetie. I'll take you home."

Luisa was efficiently bundled up and seated in Madeline's Prius in record time. She had parked her own vehicle sideways in our driveway, within a cat's whisker of our

Bronco. She handed me the keys to her car through the passenger window with an apologetic moue. "I was just so upset."

"The Bronco has its share of bumps and scrapes," Madeline said. "But it'd be a shame to put a ding in that little thing."

The "little thing" was a Mercedes 450 SL canvas top. Luisa glanced at it indifferently. "A bribe from Mamma." A pale smile touched her lips. "Mamma always gets a return on her dollar. I'm chained to the tasting room for the summer. At least I'm not teaching those freakin' cheese-making classes for the rest of the year. Caterina pulled that short stick out of the pile."

Madeline gunned the motor. I stepped back to allow them to leave, then followed them across the village to the house on Crescent in the Mercedes. Normally, I rue the invention of the combustion engine; like the cell phone, it is a piece of technology man would be better off without. But the little car was a revelation. I was almost sorry to leave it in the Brandstetters' driveway. Madeline left the Prius at the curb, and the two of them got out and walked slowly up the weedy sidewalk to the porch. I joined them. The living room lights were on, despite the fact that we were still at the gloaming part of the day.

Luisa looked at the lights, stopped short, and gasped. "He's home! I can't . . . I won't. Oh! Madeline, please, please come in with me!"

Madeline gave her a firm shove and said cheerfully, "We're right behind you!"

Neville heard us, of course, and was waiting in front of the fireplace as the three of us walked in the door. Rather, Madeline and I walked in. Luisa cracked the door, peered around the edge, cried "Neville?" in that little-girl voice, then ran forward and flung herself into his arms, kicking the little beagle aside in the process. "I thought they'd locked you up and thrown away the key!"

Neville gazed at us over the top of his wife's head. I couldn't put a name to the expression on his face, but Madeline did later, after we had gotten home. She said it was depressed and loving resignation.

"Thank you, Austin, Madeline," he said.

"No trouble at all," I said.

Neville addressed the dark head huddled in his chest. "Sweetheart, it's been a rough day. I want you to go upstairs and lie down for a bit. Do you think you can sleep?"

"She's had four good slugs of brandy," Madeline said. "She ought to be out like a light in thirty seconds flat. Come on, Luisa. Let's get you upstairs."

115

I waited until the two women had disappeared around the bend in the staircase, then I sat down in the same chair I'd occupied not six hours before. It seemed like six weeks. The beagle sniffed around my knees, looking for Lincoln. "You went down to the station and spoke with Simon?"

"Yes." Neville put his hands in his pockets and took them out again. "Yes, I did."

"That course in parasitology you teach. Was it a lecture day this morning? Or a field day?"

On a field day, the professor generally turns the class over to a TA and is free to pursue other activities. Neville's expression gave me the answer I needed.

"What did Provost have to say about that?"

He pulled his lips back in an attempt at a smile. "Not to leave town."

"Did you retain a lawyer?"

"Do you think I should?"

I looked at him for a long, grim moment. "Did you do it?"

"No. No, Austin, I didn't."

"Your innocence not withstanding, you should probably think about a lawyer."

He nodded. Then he said, "What about this Provost? Is he up to finding out who did kill Staples?"

"Undoubtedly," I said. "He is an excellent detective."

"But these last two murders in Summersville. You gave him a hand in solving those, didn't you?"

I was silent. Neville was a friend of mine. A former colleague. The stakes were very high.

"Can I hire you to look into this?"

"Of course, Neville. I will do my best. Now isn't the time, you've had quite a long day. . . ."

He barked with laughter. "A long day. If that's not a classic McKenzie understatement!"

". . . But we should sit down and discuss this tomorrow. My investigators and I" — and I confess to a feeling of pride as I said this! — "will be at the dairy on Monday, and we will be there for as long as it takes. Tomorrow is Sunday. And we will take the time to develop a plan."

The beagle ran to the foot of the stairs and looked up, tail wagging eagerly, as Madeline descended. I joined the beagle.

"Just as I thought," Madeline said. "She fell right asleep. If she's not used to brandy, Neville, she might have a head in the mornin'. You give her lots of tomato juice and aspirin." She looked up into his face.

"And you, you take care of yourself, you hear? You're going to need one cool head in this household. Now, if you'll excuse us, Austin and I will be getting on home."

Once in Madeline's Prius, my wife turned to me and said, "Somebody, Austin, ought to give that woman a slap up the side of the head. You know she's convinced that Neville killed that milk inspector because he's crazy jealous. She thinks it's her duty to let Simon know. Her own husband!" She put the car in gear with a jerk. "I swear to goodness. And he has a perfectly good alibi." She looked quickly at me. "Doesn't he?"

I evaded a direct response. "He says he's innocent. I believe him."

We drove home in silence, ruminative on my part, indignant on Madeline's.

We returned to a darkened house. Lincoln was waiting at his usual post by the back steps. Juno the Akita was prone to roaming the countryside; Ally had left her inside the house and she began a joyful barking when Madeline went inside. Lincoln and I remained out in the soft evening air. I had a habit of one last round of the barn and animals before I went to bed, and I set off now to check on our resident animals.

Ally had bedded Sunny the Hackney down in a stall next to Pony. They both greeted me with an impatient snort. August is a month of both heat and flies, and we have a practice of turning the animals out in the pasture at night and keeping them in during the day. Ally's half-bred Trakehner and our elderly Quarterhorse Andrew were grazing happily in the paddock off the barn, but Pony — a Shetland of bossy disposition and with a penchant for escape — had been conscripted to keep Sunny company. Pony shoved her nose against the stall mesh and blew out at me. This is the equine equivalent of "good evening," so I leaned against the mesh and blew back. I checked the meds sheet hanging on Sunny's stall. The last dose of bute for the day was listed in Ally's neat handwriting. Sunny shuffled over. Her gait seemed at little easier, and the worried look around her eyes had disappeared. She nosed the mesh, expecting a treat. I apologized. But her diet would have to continue. The handful of carrots I'd picked up from the tack room supply was forbidden for a few more weeks.

Outside the barn, the moon sailed high and silver, spreading its pale light over the grounds. I went to the paddock gate and whistled. There was a rumble of hooves, and Tracker and Andrew came up to the gate. Horses are tactile creatures. Andrew leaned over the fence and nudged me affectionately. Tracker nudged him, then put her neck over his and nibbled his ear. They had no objection to sharing the carrot.

Neville Brandstetter would have been better off with a horse.

FIVE

I am fond of Sundays in August. Both Madeline and Lincoln feel the heat, and the coolest place on the farm is under the willow by the duck pond. We take our meals there, and when Neville came over midmorning, I conducted file CC005's first interview with the Muscovy ducks at my feet, squabbling over the remains of my breakfast croissant.

"Madeline not going to join us?" Neville settled into the Adirondack chair with an air of taking refuge.

"She and Joe are canning beans. Allegra is on call at the clinic." I had a yellow pad and pen to hand. I dated the top of the first sheet, listed the case file number, and looked over my spectacles at Neville. "They will join us for lunch. It would be well, I think, to begin with some background on the dairy. I am particularly interested in Doucetta."

Neville stretched back in the chair and gazed up through the willow leaves at the sky, which was blue. The air was filled with sunshine. "Ah yes. Doucetta." He sat up and said briskly, "Tre Sorelle milks five hundred does and produces a rolling average of about two hundred thousand gallons of milk a year. The average is just under a gallon of milk per animal. It's an excellent average and a well-run operation. Half of the milk is sold to other processors. The rest goes into the Tre Sorelle cheeses, five hundred pounds a month."

I tried to recall the ratio of milk to cheese. My dairy classes had been nearly fifty years ago! I believe it is several pounds of milk to one pound of cheese; the ratio may differ with the type of cheese being made. I could have asked Neville, of course, but the man was in full spate.

"The cheeses are marketed all over the United States. And money comes in from the retail operation, of course. Have you ever been in it? Tre Sorelle cheeses aren't a tenth of what sells in there. She carries Swinford wines and boatloads of that touristy crap like cheese plates and picnic baskets, whatever. You go in there on a Sunday afternoon like this one, and you can't get near the register. And then there are the tours. Doucetta picked up some old draft horse at an auction and Marietta tools tourists around the hundred acres in a farm cart at fifteen dollars a head. It all adds up to quite a pile of money. Doucetta's of the old school. The company's privately held and the only other people who know what the profits really are, are God and her accountant. And I'm not too sure about the accountant."

"This is a complex business to run. Does she have advisors?"

Neville shook his head. "Just the firm that does the taxes. And I swear, Austin, she's got a second set of books somewhere. The retail business brings in a lot of cash. She's not real big on reporting the income, but she's the kind of personality that needs to track every nickel. She came over from Italy when she was sixteen. Had an arranged marriage with the old man — Dominic, his name was, and he passed away when Luisa was just a kid. There were three daughters: Luisa's the youngest by more than ten years; then there was Margarita, who died of a stroke a couple of years ago; and Caterina, the oldest. Caterina remembers the old man; he was quiet, she said. I got the impression that when Doucetta said "jump" the old man jumped and asked if it was high enough. Margarita had one daughter, Marietta. Her husband just up and disappeared a few years after Marietta was born. He died sometime after that — in Italy, I think.

"Marietta herself went on to Vassar, got a good degree there, and went from that to an MBA at the Wharton School. She's probably the best candidate as a successor to Doucetta, and the old lady dotes on her — as much as the old lady dotes on anybody.

"Caterina married a guy named Frank Celestine. A real jerk, if you want to know the truth, and a lazy one at that. If you're looking for suspects based on who deserves to be locked up on general principles, take a good hard look at Frank. Caterina herself isn't as dumb as she makes out, and she's certainly not as scatterbrained as she appears, but living with someone like Frank would suppress anybody's natural personality, and hers wasn't all that definite to begin with. The old lady dominates all of them. Which is why Caterina's forced to put up with Frank. Doucetta doesn't believe in divorce. As a mother — well, she's terrorized all of them since they were kids, and I suppose Caterina doesn't know anything else. You know how chickens will pick one poor bird out of the flock and peck it senseless? That's how Doucetta and Frank treat

Caterina.

"Anyway, Frank and Caterina have two sons. Neither one of them was interested in the dairy. As a matter of fact, I think they both went to Italy to live ten or twelve years ago. There were some rumblings about drugs when they left. Maybe a felony or two. I don't know the details.

"And, as you know, Luisa and I didn't have any children at all. It looks as if Marietta's the only family member available to take over the dairy when Doucetta dies. Have you met her?"

I shook my head.

"Beautiful girl. Of course, all of Doucetta's offspring are beautiful. She's a stock-broker, or was. She came back from New York to help out a couple of years ago. She's got the brains to take the dairy over, that's for sure. Whether she has the desire is anybody's guess. But other than Marietta — there's nobody."

We were both silent, looking over the duck pond. I had married late in life, astounding my colleagues who had thought me a con-firmed bachelor at fifty. The children Madeline and I both wished for had not come. But our lives had been enriched by the long procession of students who had eaten at our table and become part of our lives for the time they had been at school.

"At any rate, Doucetta runs the place with an iron fist, or cane rather. Have you seen that goat-headed stick she carries? Of course you have, you were there when she thumped Abrahamson in the shins at the guild meeting. The kids are all petrified of her. And she keeps the purse strings open just enough so that it'd take real character to walk away from the place."

"At ninety-four," I began.

"Yes. At ninety-four, Doucetta's not immortal. I don't know who'll take over the operation after she goes. Nobody does. Caterina's husband probably has big ideas, but the guy's a real loser. She never got past sixth grade, Doucetta didn't. She combines this amazing genius for business with peasant superstitions." He tugged his beard. "My guess, the whole thing will dwindle away once she's gone. In the meantime, she keeps the milk right on coming."

"I'm surprised no one's offered to buy her out. One of the big cheese companies, perhaps."

"It'd make sense," Neville said. "But I don't know a thing about it. Doucetta had me doing the necessary vet work at the dairy when Luisa and I were first married, but I haven't set foot in the place for years — nor have I talked to Doucetta other than Christmas and birthdays."

"When did you stop treating the goats?"

"Most of us drop clinical in favor of the teaching and research. You know that better than anybody does. But even if I had kept up private practice, I couldn't have worked with her. We crossed swords early on. She's got notions about handling animals I don't approve of . . . and don't want to know about, frankly."

I wasn't sure whether I should pursue this lead at the moment, or not. If Doucetta were engaging in unseemly practices, I would see that for myself. I made a brief note and said, "Which brings us to the high somatic cell count."

"Yeah, I thought we'd get there." Neville tugged at his beard with both hands. "I'll tell you what I think, Austin. I think it's sabotage."

I was somewhat nonplussed. "By whom? And why? Or perhaps my first question should be: Are you sure? Broadly speaking, the cytokines critical in the early recruitment of PMN to the mammary gland are created in response to mastitis pathogens. Are there cases of mastitis in the Tre Sorelle goats?"

"It's truer for cows than goats," Neville

127

said. "Estrus, season, and milk yield raise the cell count in goats. Even the breed and the geographic area can affect the count in goats. Everyone has had a guess at why. Nobody's got much on how to fix it."

"Troublesome," I said. "And quite interesting." My primary contribution to animal research had been a series of landmark studies on bovine back fat. To be truthful, at the time of my retirement, the subspecialty had been pretty well mined out. This area of caprine study was new to me. And intriguing. "Is anyone engaged in field studies?"

"Everybody who's anybody in the field is having a whack at it," Neville said. "But you know the problems with funding."

How well I knew the problems of funding!

"The Europeans have a lot more going on than we do, at the moment. More goats over there."

"And you say some breeds seem more prone to the problem than others?"

"Apparently. But we haven't any definitive studies yet."

"I'm more familiar with the meat goat breeds," I admitted. "Savannas, Boers, and of course, the ubiquitous Spanish. The dairy has Saanens, primarily?" Saanens are known for producing a gallon of milk a day with dependable regularity.

"Saanens, Toggs, and Alpines."

"Toggenburgs," I said. "An attractive goat, if memory serves. But not a great deal of butter fat, surely?"

"There's exceptions to every rule, Austin. Researchers know that better than anyone does. For a while there, Doucetta played around with outcrossing, trying to create a breed that'd combine the best characteristics of the standards and eliminate the worst, but she couldn't see an immediate return, so she stopped. She's a cash-on-the-nail-head kind of lady."

"You suspect sabotage, you said? There must be surer ways of putting her out of business."

"With so many variables affecting the MSCC in goats, who's to say it isn't just bad luck? It'd be hard to catch somebody who's clever at it. You don't even believe it."

"You do, apparently."

"That's right. I do. And since you've got that look in your eye, all I can tell you is that it just doesn't feel right. The pattern's too persistent. There's no fluctuation in the readings. They're consistently a hundred thousand over a million. And there should be fluctuation. The only set of conditions I know of at the moment that reliably produces a higher count is mastitis, and there isn't any. All the other factors would give you an up and down count from sample to sample." Neville got up and moved restlessly around the lawn. "As for why — well, Doucetta's made a lot of enemies in her lifetime. Aren't there supposed to be three basic motives for crime? Greed, lust, and revenge? Thanks to Doucetta, the dairy's awash in 'em."

I mused. There was a great deal to think about. The yellow pad in my lap was covered with notes, including double underlines, which indicated those possible motives.

Greed. Lust. Revenge.

"I see Madeline," Neville said, with the cheerful note that almost always attends those who speak of my wife. "And she's carrying lunch!"

I set the yellow pad aside. I was as ready as I could be for my appearance at the scene of the crime tomorrow.

And I hadn't the least notion of where to begin.

Six

"And what do you think you're doing here, arsehole?" Doucetta stood at the dairy door, feet planted wide, with cane held crosswise to bar my team from entry.

The morning was not beginning well.

It was seven thirty, and the air was thick with the bleats of does waiting for their turn in the milking. A light rain was falling on the Tre Sorelle Dairy. Although I had passed by the place many times, I had never actually been on the premises.

It was even more impressive close up than from the roadside.

The dairy buildings and creamery formed a T that was at right angles to the long metal shed barns that housed the goats. The office and the milking parlor formed the bar of the T and faced the courtyard; the creamery where the cheese was made formed the shank. Both the house on the hillside overlooking the dairy and dairy buildings were constructed of pale pink stucco now dampened slightly with the misty rain. Building maintenance in a commercial farming operation is a continuous problem and frequently neglected. I was impressed to see that the worn spots in the stucco were neatly patched. One of the long wrought-iron sconces was detached from the wall near the office door and the wall patching was in process, but at least the work was being done.

Wisteria wound around the eaves and the window jambs. The drive — more of a courtyard if one considered the fountain chiming in the center of the brick paving — was swept and free of detritus. The heavy flower scent mingled pleasantly with the odor of goat.

"Madam," I said. "As I have explained — exhaustively — we have been sent by the university and the State of New York to assess the vulnerability of your dairy operation to pathogens inciting the rise in your somatic cell count."

I could not have been clearer if I'd written out our mission on a chalkboard. Yet the confounded woman refused us entry!

Her fierce black eyes had the steady, unwavering glare of a lioness stalking warthogs. It was most unsettling. She turned them to Leslie Chou, who was cowering behind me. "This arsehole speaks English?"

"Yes, ma'am." She poked her head over my shoulder. "We're just here to look. Honestly."

Joseph, who had been watching this scene unfold with a very regrettable twinkle in his eye, said, "We're just here to offer some help, ma'am." Then, to my astonishment he said, *"Il mio capo è testardo, ma una brava persona."*

She slammed the point of the cane on the stoop and took a step forward. She squinted at Joe's dark hair. "You Italian?" she said suspiciously. *"Che cosa fa un bravo regazzo come te con undisgraziato simile?"*

My Italian was limited to a crash course I took when Madeline and I had gone to Rome on our honeymoon. But I believe Joe had told her I was as obstinate as a pig, and that she had asked him what a nice boy like him was doing with a . . . person . . . like me. I cleared my throat in a meaningful way.

Joe shot me an apologetic glance. "I do speak Italian. My grandmother, *donna,* on my mother's side."

"You are here to pee in my milk and make it bad for the test!"

"No, *donna,* we're here to help you."

She snorted. She sucked her lower lip with

a very unpleasant sound. Then she said, "Okay. You come in." She shook the cane at me. "But you speak English!"

Her first request, with which I thoroughly concurred, was to wear clear plastic over-shoes to minimize the conveyance of any outside contaminants. Farm animals have varying immunity to a wide variety of infectious complaints that can be carried from barn to barn. Sore mouth, foot rot, and caseous lymphadenitis — not to mention pneumonia and bacteria-borne abscesses — are among the most dangerous. An unhappy goat gives far less milk.

Her second, third, and fourth requests were to shut up and speak English. Fortunately, Joe's Italian was up to the task of translating both my questions and her answers. Despite the fact that I knew she understood me quite well, our discussion took considerably more time than necessary. I felt as if I were playing Ping-Pong.

For some reason, perhaps due to an understandable case of nerves, young Leslie Chou was afflicted with a severe case of giggles throughout the tour.

I find well-run dairy operations very happy places to be. Good sanitation dictates a heavy use of concrete in construction. All the equipment is heavy-gauge stainless steel, except for the hoses, which are thick PVC plastic. A well-run dairy is always cool and slightly damp, like a grotto behind a waterfall. Unlike cattle, goats rarely pass manure in the milking parlor, and the entire process is very clean.

We began the tour at the milking parlor.

Goats are talkative creatures, particularly in comparison with cows, and the does conducted quite a conversation among themselves as they ambled into the parlor from the holding pen. One by one, Doucetta's employees, who appeared to be Mexican gentlemen, cleansed the does' udders with a disinfectant, and then attached the inflations to their teats.

The seasoned milkers were perfectly content to stand quietly while the vacuum lines did their work. Tre Sorelle's practice was to feed the does some grain during milking and the goats munched pleasantly. The Mexican gentlemen who handled the milking paid close attention as the udders emptied of milk, to the necessity of "stripping out" the udder, that is, making sure that as much milk was removed from the mammary gland as possible. Overmilking and the subsequent damage to the teats is a frequent contributor to mastitis. It did not seem to be a problem here. Each gentleman disinfected each teat with an iodine dip.

The care of raw milk — be it bovine, caprine, or ovine, has the same basic steps. The milk is collected and cooled to 38 degrees Fahrenheit with agitator paddles. If it is to be used raw, it is pumped into canisters and put straight into the cooler. It is heated to 185 degrees if it is to be pasteurized, and then stored in a refrigerated space. At large dairies, the entire process is automated from beginning to end. We observed each step of the process closely. In the milk room, I paid particular attention to the scene of the crime. A yellow police tape surrounded the middle tank. Doucetta jerked her thumb at it and snarled at me, "All that milk. Gone. Down the drain. That *carabinari* owes me some big check."

I assumed she meant the Summersville Police Department. I decided not to pass the request on to Provost.

I made a quick sketch of the room's layout. The room was a rectangle, about sixty feet long by forty feet wide. The bulk tanks sat in the middle. There was a door at each end of the length, one to the outside office, the other to the milking parlor.

At the close of milking, we observed the cleansing process. There are four dairy cleaning agents mandated by both state law and common sense: alkaline and acid detergents for cleansing, and iodine and chlorine for sanitizing. All the equipment was washed with tepid water and an alkaline cleaner, followed by hot water and an acid cleaner, to avoid a buildup of casein, a by-product of milk. Finally, there is a chlorine santizer cold-water rinse.

Were milking goats an Olympic competition, Tre Sorelle would have scored a ten.

There was one other thing worthy of note. On the parlor and the milk room side, the dairy emptied out completely once the milking and the cleanup were finished. The three workers went on to their assignments at the creamery and that side of the dairy was totally deserted, until milking began again.

Doucetta led us back to the dairy office. Ashley Swinford, who apparently needed very little time to recuperate from her discovery of the body, was back at her desk. She wore a Tre Sorelle T-shirt, white jeans, and a flirtatious smile for Joe.

Doucetta planted herself in front of me. Despite the pugnacity exhibited by her out-thrust jaw, I sensed that she was eager for my opinion.

"Please tell Mrs. Capretti that I am most impressed with the professionalism of her dairy," I said to Joe.

This apparently needed no translation. "Told you, arsehole," Doucetta said. "My milk is perfect."

"Just to be on the safe side, there is one other potential source of contaminants, and that is the feed," I said. "Joe, would you please ask Mrs. Capretti if we may take samples of the grain and hay? I'll send them up to Cornell to be tested."

Doucetta laughed skeptically. But she nodded agreement.

"I'll get it," Leslie said. "If that's okay with you, Mrs. C."

"Go," Doucetta said. Leslie went but not, I noticed, before she cast a worshipful glance at Joe and a worried look at Ashley's blonde magnificence.

"And we will walk the pastures, if you please," I said. "The caprine autoimmune system . . ."

English! Doucetta shouted.

"A lot of weeds are poisonous to goats," I said.

"We have no such weeds," Doucetta said flatly. "If we do have such weeds, some snake put them there. You, maybe."

"Madam, I assure you —"

"You know what?" Ashley interrupted brightly. "I'll bet Marietta would haul you guys around the pasture in the farm cart. They've got more than five hundred acres, Dr. McKenzie. It'll take you all day if you walk. We don't run tours on Monday, so she'll just be hanging around anyhow. Shall I call her down, Mrs. C.?"

"Call her," Doucetta said. "Let him take the tour. Let him see if he can find one single thing wrong with my land. Ptoo!" And she spit.

Then she steadied herself on her cane and held out her hand. At last, a gesture of goodwill. I took it and shook it heartily. Doucetta snatched it back. "Forty-five bucks," she said.

"I beg your pardon?"

"The tour costs fifteen dollars a head. There are three of you. Three times fifteen is forty-five dollars." She thrust her hand under my nose. "Fork it over." She gave me an evil smile. "Fork it over. That is a colloquialism. My English is a little better than yours is, maybe? For example, I do not say . . ." She puffed up her chest and said self-importantly, "There is a primary cost associated with the transportations of a person or persons around the environs of our establishment. I say: the tour is fifteen dollars American. Each. Eleven-fifty in euros. We do not accept pesos. Fork it over, arsehole." She swung her cane up and poked me in the chest. "English!"

Just then, Leslie came back with a plastic bag of grain and hay samples, the sample bottles, and the CMT tally sheet. Ashley and Marietta followed her. These timely arrivals prevented me from uttering a most ungentlemanly imprecation.

This granddaughter of Doucetta's was tall and slender, with a cloud of exquisite black hair and an aquiline nose. Joe, who had been slouched against the desk, straightened up with an audible snap as she came into the room. I am not good at women's ages — it would be a lot handier if one were allowed to examine their teeth — but she seemed to be in her midthirties, despite the fact that there were no lines at all in her smooth complexion.

Marietta greeted me courteously, dismissed Leslie with a flick of her long eyelashes, and proceeded to dissuade her grandmother from extortion. We went outside to wait for her to fetch the horse, who turned out to be a pleasant, strong old fellow named Pete. Joe gave her a hand with the harness, and we were soon aboard.

I sat beside her on the perch seat of the wagon. Joe, Ashley, and Leslie sat along the benches in back. "It all depends on your approach," Marietta said, when I thanked her for driving us gratis. "Grandmamma thinks that everyone's a crook and if they aren't crooks, they're out to take advantage. Probably," she added affably, "because she's a crook and she's an ace at squeezing the last nickel out of the tourists."

"A crook?" I said, alertly.

"Oh, just the usual stuff, you know. A lot of the store receipts are in cash, for instance. Most of that doesn't see the inside of a bank account, much less show up as taxable income. My aunt Caterina handles the bookkeeping and it drives her bananas. And haven't you noticed it's the people who *are* something — like crooked or out for themselves — that think other people are, too?"

"You may have a point."

More to the point was why this exceptionally pretty woman was being so forthright with me about her grandmother's accounting practices. Mentally, I filed that away under Items to Mull Over While Drinking Scotch.

We drove out of the driveway and down the dirt road that ran through Tre Sorelle lands. There were tightly fenced pastures on either side. The milking does had been herded out of the barn and through a steel-sided lane that led directly to the two front pastures. Happy goats graze with their tails straight up in the air. Like puppies, they wag them when particularly pleased. The does in these pastures appeared more than content.

We drew up to the first gate and stopped. Ashley jumped out of the back, opened the gate, and ushered us through. She closed it behind the cart and resumed her seat.

Marietta shook the reins and the very well-put-together Percheron broke into a jog trot. "Any particular place in this pasture where you want to start?"

"Is there a stream?"

She nodded toward the hedgerow that bifurcated this pasture from the one adjacent.

"Let's begin there."

If the does drank from a marsh, there was a distinct danger of coccidiosis infection in the herd. But I put paid to this notion when I saw the water wagon parked by the stream's edge. This equipment is quite useful when raising stock on pasture. The wagon is loaded with a thousand-gallon tank of water. The water runs through a gravity hose to a stock tank on the ground. It is a simple and effective way to get clean water to stock. The tank was free of mold and algae and manure. The water looked clear enough for humans to drink, although we would take samples of all of it.

We descended from the wagon. Joe, dogged by Ashley and Marietta, went to the water tank and then the stream to take samples. Leslie and I split up, and walked along either side of the small stream checking for noxious weeds. Goats are susceptible to a wide variety of toxins: rue, wild cherry, yew, all the nightshades, nettles, vetch — the list is extensive. Perhaps the most dangerous is bracken fern, which acts on the central nervous system and gives the animal a case of the blind staggers. Tre Sorelle's pastures consisted mainly of timothy, clover, dandelions, purple nettle, borage, fescue, and a bit of alfalfa. There was the occasional multiflora rose or honeysuckle bush that had not yet succumbed to the caprines' voracious browsing habits. We spot searched that pasture, and the seven beyond it.

We found nothing poisonous at all.

We returned to the dairy sometime well after three o'clock. My case was filled with samples of grasses, weeds, and water. Good research dictated that we run the appropriate tests, but I doubted that anything of significance would turn up.

"Back at square one," Joe said as he unkinked himself from the wagon ride.

"Very likely," I agreed. "It's a pretty little problem, isn't it?" I sat down on a decoratively painted milk can.

Joe put his hand on my shoulder. "You look hungry, Doc. We missed lunch, didn't we?"

I admitted to a desire for lunch.

Marietta backed the wagon to its usual parking spot. At the sound of the Percheron's hooves clattering on the pavers, the door to the dairy opened and Doucetta stamped onto the stoop. She waved her cane, presumably to get my attention. "Hey! Arsehole!"

"Grandmamma." Marietta turned from loosening the bit and shook her head at the old lady. "I just spent the afternoon with Dr. McKenzie and he's a perfectly nice old man. Stop calling him names."

Old man? I looked sternly at the woman over my spectacles.

Doucetta stamped a little farther down the steps. "So? Did you find poison in my pastures?"

I shook my head. "We've taken samples, Mrs. Capretti. But your pastures appear to be in excellent shape."

"I told you so."

Joe shut the rear hatch on the Bronco and

144

came over to stand by me. *"Donna,"* he said. "You run a great place here. You know your goats. Why do you think the tests are coming back the way they are?"

"Finally," she said. "Somebody has the brains to ask *me.* All of you big important people are running around blabber, blabber, blabber. Test this. Test that. But nobody asks me."

She was right. Perhaps because she was so old, perhaps because she was foreign, perhaps because she was female, we had overlooked the most important source of information about the goats. Madeline was right. I had a great many prejudices to set aside. "My apologies, madam," I said.

"A madam," she snapped, "is the boss of a whorehouse, right? I am not your madam. As for my goats?" She thrust two fingers in the air and muttered, *"Maledizione."*

"Cursed?" Joe said.

"Ever since my grandsons were driven from this land," she said dramatically, "there has been a curse on this place!"

Marietta shook her head. "You don't really believe that, Grandmamma."

"Do I not? Have all the scientists and other nosy people who have butted into my business told me otherwise?"

"No," I admitted, "we have not. But if you

are cursed, madam, it is through a man-made agency. And I promise you, we will get to the bottom of this."

Doucetta muttered something Joe refused to translate. Then she retreated to the dairy office and slammed the door.

I sat back down on the milk can to think.

"You *are* tired, Dr. McKenzie," Leslie said with concern. "Can I get you something cold to drink?"

"I am not sitting down because I am tired, I am merely taking the opportunity to reflect," I said testily. "I am perfectly capable of beginning all over again from the top."

"I don't think starting over'd get us anywhere, though," Leslie said. "I can't find a place to go from here except for the goats themselves, and that doesn't seem likely. They look perfectly fit. She doesn't keep on the older milkers. She culls the herd for malformed teats and low production. She staggers the kidding, too. This is all totally by the book." She looked at the neat barns, the well-kept buildings, the closely shaved lawn, and the pots of bright pink geraniums. She rattled the wrought-iron sconce that still hadn't been replaced on the building. "This is a fabulous place. It's heaven."

"For goats," Marietta said dryly. She slipped a halter over the Perch's head and clipped his lead line to the hitching post. "And if you can handle the fact that the nearest Barneys is three hundred miles due south." Her eyes flickered over Leslie's garb; the young student was dressed in khaki shorts, work boots, and a T-shirt that read "Goats Are Great."

"Yeah, well, you can see how far into Barneys I am," Leslie said with a grin. "Now, if you're talking Lincoln Center, I'm your woman."

"What's Barneys?" Ashley asked.

The ensuing conversation between the three women was close to incomprehensible to me. Joe began to pack up the Bronco preparatory to our departure. I sat on the milk can and looked over the notes I'd taken throughout the day. We would come back to take random samples of the does' milk, but I was reasonably certain Neville's suggestion of sabotage was becoming a real possibility. But who? And why?

If the sabotage was connected to Melvin Staples's murder — as it surely must be — what deadly knowledge did poor Melvin have?

SEVEN

"Beats me what he was up to," Mrs. Staples said.

After a restorative hamburger and onion rings at the Embassy, Leslie headed back to her student digs in Ithaca, and Joe and I stopped by the Staples's home to see what information could be gleaned from the widow.

Kelly Staples was a short, compact woman with cropped brown hair and a direct manner. Two toddlers wound themselves around her legs. There were circles under her eyes, and she was pale under her summer tan, but she was composed and readily agreed to discuss the case with us.

The house was a neatly kept bungalow in that section of Summersville where real estate prices remain modest. The living room was small, with a wide-screen TV in one corner and a couch in a blue tweed sort of fabric opposite. The brown-and-white carpet had the texture of a sheepdog's winter coat. The place was littered with toys. As we sat down, an older woman came in from what must have been the kitchen and took the youngsters away with her.

"Thanks, Ma." Kelly rubbed her forehead a little wearily. "I was on a sleepover with her in Syracuse when I heard Mel passed. She came back with me to help with the kids. Usually we fight like cats and dogs. But she's been a real help, especially with all this funeral stuff."

"The body's been released, then?" I said.

"What? Mel, you mean? Yeah. That Provost called me around lunchtime."

"Excellent," I said. This meant the forensics report and the autopsy would be available to Simon, and, therefore, to me.

Mrs. Staples looked suspiciously at me. "What'n the heck you mean by that?"

"What Dr. McKenzie means is that it's excellent you don't have to wait around to make the arrangements for Mr. Staples's . . . passing," Joe said. There was a particular politeness to Joe's tones that I had begun to notice on more than one occasion. When we had visited the Swinford barns, for example. And he had interceded in just that way when Doucetta swelled up like an irate cobra over a perfectly simple request to pull

149

samples from the bulk tanks. Curious.

"You may know that Neville Brandstetter has retained my firm to investigate the murder of your husband," I said. "We . . ."

"I thought you two were vets."

"We are. Well, Joseph is a third-year."

"A veterinarian's investigating Mel's passing? Is it because he works for the ag and markets department?"

"Mrs. Staples, I am a detective."

She looked confused. "Okay," she said uncertainly. "You were asking if Mel'd been acting kind of weird lately? Yeah. He was. And I didn't know what he was up to, although knowing Mel, it was probably some woman."

"Some woman," I repeated, mainly to gain some time to consider how to form the next question. "Women were a frequent distraction for Mr. Staples?"

"Call him Mel," she said, "everybody called him Mel. Blondes, brunettes, redheads."

Jealousy. The oldest motive of all. It was Iago who called it "the green-eyed monster." It had doomed many a poor soul.

"You don't seem all that upset by it," Joe suggested tactfully.

She shrugged. "The way he explained it, with some guys, it's motorcycles. With others, stock-car racing. This was a lot less dangerous."

"More or less a hobby of his, then," I ventured.

She brightened. "Yeah. That way it doesn't sound too bad, does it? I mean, I have to tell you, at the beginning, it kind of sent me off the deep end, you know? I was fit to spit. But then, well, look at him." She rose from the recliner where she had been sitting and went to an étagère kind of affair against the wall. "Here." She picked up a photograph and thrust it at me.

I had never seen Melvin Staples alive. He resembled that short, crazy Australian who so disastrously attempted *Hamlet* some years ago. Although Staples appeared much taller.

"You see those eyes?" Kelly asked somewhat rhetorically. "Women just went apeshit for him."

"But he always came back to you?" Joe said.

"Yep." Her confidence was absolute. "Loved me, loved the kiddies."

Of the many locutions I despise, "kiddies" is chief among them. I sighed. Then I said, "I truly don't wish to distress you, Mrs. Staples. But if I were to tell you that Melvin seems to have made arrangements to move in with one of his lady friends, it would seem to belie his pledge of constancy."

"Huh?"

"He was shacking up with an older woman," Joe said bluntly.

She furrowed her brow. "You mean that ditso Mrs. Brandstetter?" She sat up a little. "Hey! You said a guy named Brandstetter hired you? Any relation?"

"Her husband."

"You can tell Mrs. Cradle Robber that Mel was in it for the money. She's fifty if she's a day, for cripes' sake." She sat on the edge of the recliner and bent forward in a confiding way. "She was going to give Mel that Mercedes she drives. You seen that thing?" She sat back, triumphant. "She might have already done that. In that case, I'd get it, wouldn't I?"

I bit my mustache. Madeline wasn't there to tell me not to do it, so I bit it again.

"Lieutenant Provost said that someone sent you pictures of Mrs. Brandstetter and your husband through the mail?" Joe asked. "Was there any kind of demand associated with them?"

Suddenly, the woman became very shifty. She looked away from me and out the living room window. "Nah."

"They just came out of the blue?" I said. "I find that very curious, Mrs. Staples."

Joe leaned against the wall, his arms folded. He reminded me of someone. Philip Marlowe, that was it. If he'd had a fedora, he could have been the great detective's double. "You took those photographs, didn't you, Kelly? If you didn't get the Mercedes from Mrs. Brandstetter, you were going to hit up her husband."

She licked her lips. "There's no law against that."

"There is most certainly a law against blackmail," I said sternly.

"You!" she said, with swift viciousness. "Like you can't afford anything you want. People like you get treated a lot different from people like us. You know how hard it is to get a break these days? I'm telling you this, Dr. McKenzie, if we hadn't gotten a break on the taxes on this place, me and my kids would be out in the street!"

"A break on your taxes," I repeated.

"Yeah. Like I said, Mel was up to something and whatever it was, he wasn't about to tell me."

"Up to something with whom?"

She looked surprised. "That tax inspector. Brian Folk." She made her hands "talk" to one another. "He and Mel were *pst, pst, pst,* like two little old ladies all the time. Whatever they were up to, that Brian sure gave us a break with the assessment." She looked sulky. "Of course, now that Mel's passed I suppose the blessed taxes'll go up again. And it'll be a cold day in the hot place before I get my hands on that Mercedes, I suppose." She sighed sentimentally. "Poor old Mel. His timing was always rotten."

The younger of the two children came listing into the living room. He was rapidly followed by his sibling. There was an acrimonious discussion over a red plastic truck. Over the ensuing shrieks, Joseph and I prepared to take our leave. I turned to her as we headed out the door. "Was it unusual for your husband to work a six-day week?"

"You mean how come he was out at the dairy on a Saturday?"

"Yes. He had taken a third sample of milk earlier in the week. Did he say anything to you about why he was at the dairy again?"

"Who knows? Maybe he was trying to stick it to the old hag that runs the place. She's a real terror, that one."

We said our good-byes, although I found it very hard to remain courteous as we did so.

Once in the car, we both leaned back in the seats and exhaled.

"She's something else." Joe shook his head. "It never occurred to me to wonder why he was back at the dairy so soon. Do you think it's important?"

"I don't know."

He put the key in the ignition. "Where to now, Doc?"

"I think I need to let Provost know about the blackmail attempt. It may be a significant factor in the investigation."

Madeline and Lila Gernsback had a standing date to go swimming at the high school on Monday nights, and she wouldn't be back until nine o'clock or so. There was a cold supper waiting in the refrigerator for Joe and me at home. I was eager to hear Simon's reaction to the interview with Kelly Staples, so I dropped Joe off at the house and went on to the police station in the hope that he hadn't left for the day. My luck was in. I summarized the results of my interviews to date, ending with the curious fact of the low assessment.

"Brian Folk gave the Staples's a break on their assessment? That has to break some kind of state law, doesn't it?" Provost looked expectantly at me, then pulled open the lower drawer of his desk and thumbed through the files in its interior. He pulled out a thin manila folder and opened it up. "Federal civil laws, state criminal laws . . . Okay. Here we are. State statutes. Howie

Murchinson. This guy is an expert on the statutes around this kind of stuff. This is a Hemlock Falls number." He looked up at the clock on his office wall. "Shoot. It's after six. Do you suppose he's still there?"

"I have no idea." He punched the numbers into the phone. I reached for the week's edition of the *Sentinel,* which was lying on Provost's desk.

"That so," Simon said into the phone. Apparently, Howie Murchinson was still at his law office in Hemlock Falls and willing to answer Simon's questions about Brian Folk's tax-assessing practices. "Well, sir, I couldn't say. Not verified, no. We'll get right on it. Thank you, sir." He hung up. I looked at him expectantly.

"Nice fella, for a lawyer." Simon clasped his hands behind his head and leaned back in his chair. "But he couldn't give me a straight answer, either." He gazed ruminatively at the photograph of his wife and teenaged son prominently displayed on his desk. " 'Subjective,' he said. Unless the rate's so low it'd be obvious to a blind baboon that Folk's giving the Staples's a break. And then you have to prove bribery, which involves a lot of evidence we sure as heck don't have at the moment. But it's my impression that it can be done." He smiled beatifically. "Oh, I'd like to nail that sucker, Doc."

"A fair number of Summersvillians would appear to agree with you." I'd been perusing the *Sentinel* as Simon made his call. "Did you see Rita's editorial?"

" 'Boot on the Taxpayer's Neck'? You bet I did. She's a firecracker, that Rita."

I folded the paper and placed it back on his desk. "Other than a desire to impress his overlords in Albany, can you think of a reason why Brian Folk would be so egregious in his estimates of the value of our local property?"

"To be fair," Simon said uncomfortably, "I made some calls around the county and it looks as if Summersville's way behind on property valuation. Old Nicky Ferguson's heart was in the right place, but apparently, he wasn't very responsible. So a large part of this is the piper being paid." He leaned forward suddenly. "But I find the hanky-panky between Staples and Folk pretty interesting, don't you?"

I nodded. "It's worth exploring. Mrs. Staples said that Melvin's body has been released for burial?"

"Yep."

"So the autopsy report's complete? And I take it the scene-of-the-crime people are finished with the site. The dairy was open for business today. Which means the forensics data are available?"

Simon groaned, rubbed his hands over his face, looked from side to side as if the gods of justice were looming over his shoulder, then retrieved a file from the top of his desk and handed it to me. "And I'd appreciate it if you wouldn't make a big noise about the fact that I've passed this stuff on to you."

I'd looked immediately at the "probable weapon" box on the autopsy sheet. " 'A blunt weapon with a metal head, perhaps a ball-peen hammer with an extended handle'?" I lowered the report and looked Simon in the eye. "An oak cane with a brass goat's head, perhaps?"

Simon nodded.

"Have you confiscated the cane?"

Simon nodded again. Then he corrected himself. "Nope. I'm a liar. I got the warrant to allow us to take it in as material evidence. To be perfectly accurate, I sent Kevin Kiddermeister out to pick it up." He looked at the clock on his office wall again. "He ought to be back any minute now."

Kevin was the newest recruit in the Summersville police force. He must have drawn the short straw. "If he isn't dead." I shuddered.

"He can take care of himself," Provost said with a doubtful air. "And the Kiddermeisters have all made a career out of police work anyhow, so it's not as if I sent in a virgin sacrifice, for Pete's sake." We looked at each other. Simon said, "She's ninety-four. And she doesn't weigh more than that soaking wet." Then he said, "Maybe I better give him a call." He withdrew his cell phone from the pocket of his jacket and was about to speed-dial when there was a tap at the door and Kevin Kiddermeister walked in. Like all the Kiddermeister men, he was blond, blue-eyed, and blushed easily. He was blushing now, but he carried the cane, rather as a veteran centurion of Rome must have carried the eagle standard after a successful attack on the Gauls. And like the centurion, he carried battle scars, a lump on his jaw, to be precise. Simon made a sympathetic noise. "Clocked you one, did she?"

Kevin gave me a half salute and nodded to his chief. "Yessir. I ducked the wrong way. You told me she was right-handed? Turns out she's ambi-whatsis."

Ambidextrous. Curious, I glanced at the Nature of Wound subcategory on the autopsy report. "A right-handed perp, in any event," I said. I observed the goat-headed cane, carefully wrapped in plastic. "Well done, my boy."

Simon rose, took the cane, and locked it in the evidence cabinet. "Yep. You can get along home, now, Kevin."

"Yessir." He turned to leave and hesitated, one hand on the office door. "It's not all going to be like this, is it?"

"Could have been worse," Simon said thoughtfully. "She could have had a gun."

Kevin shut the door with a nervous bang.

I read through the reports from Syracuse. Neither the forensics nor the autopsy provided much joy. Staples's fingerprints were found outside the stainless-steel rim of the bulk tank. The thumbprints and the heel of the hand were under the rim, the fingers of both hands were inside. Brush marks on the lower half of the tank had possibly been made by someone's knees. The scenario was obvious: Staples had been struck on the head while bending over the tank, sagged against it, and been tipped over. The actual cause of death was drowning. From the amount of milk splashed on the floor around the tank, the victim had struggled a little.

"I don't see the old lady as a viable suspect," Provost said.

"Archimedes would disagree."

Provost closed his eyes, and then opened

160

them again. "I'll bite, Doc."

" 'Give me a lever and I'll move the world.' Archimedes said that, not I," I added impatiently. "It wouldn't take a huge amount of strength to tip the body into the bulk tank. If he were badly stunned — and from the description of the head wound, he would have hardly been conscious as he went under — he wouldn't have struggled much." I thought about it. What I knew about ageing was confined to the remarkable resilience of animals and the annoying changes in my own body. "Let's say it's not totally impossible." I paged through the rest of the report. "The cleanliness of the dairy is a hindrance. There are no data of note anywhere except the tank." I replaced the papers in the file and handed it back to Simon. "No witnesses. No forensics. Whatever case we make, Provost, is bound to be circumstantial."

"So it's going to come down to motive?" Simon didn't look happy. "The law likes hard fact, Doc."

I cast a glance at the cabinet that held the cane. "We may have the means. Intensive questioning of the suspects can establish opportunity. And just plain research will support the motive. There are quite a few avenues to pursue."

"You think so?" Simon demanded. "Who've we got for suspects? A ninety-four-year-old widow? A jury's going to love that."

"Then our first step should be to establish the parameters of our investigation by eliminating who is not a suspect. I may have mentioned before that a criminal investigation involves the same thought processes used in diagnosing a pathological condition."

"Yeah, Doc."

"Fact find, assess, and conclude."

"Yeah, Doc."

"Our first step is to rule out."

"Yeah, Doc." He sighed. "It'd be nice if we could rule out more chatter on the disease model."

"You mean you'd like to cut to the chase, as they say."

"You got it in one."

I leaned back in my chair and steepled my fingers. It occurred to me that it would be very pleasant to have a Scotch in my hand. "There is something to consider about this case that is very odd. An anomaly, if you will."

Simon rolled his eyes.

"Until I discover the source of the contamination of the milk, we have two issues to consider. I believe the contamination to be sabotage, designed to close the dairy down. Why close the dairy down? We have the murder of the milk inspector: the motive seems to be revenge for his womanizing, in which case the sabotage and the murder are unrelated; or his accurate reporting of the MSCC levels, that, too, would work to close the dairy down. In which case his murder and the sabotage are unconnected. Unless Staples was the saboteur. But I believe the two are connected. I just don't know how."

Provost rubbed his forehead. "I think I'm getting a headache. You mean somebody could have killed Mel out of jealousy — and somebody *else* is trying to close the dairy."

"Let's take the murder on, first. I am close to discovering the antecedents of the other problem. We will reserve a conclusion on that for a later time."

Provost shook his head, as if bothered by flies. "The murder. Yeah. Now. I don't need to tell you that most murders are committed by the vic's loved ones."

"A fact known to all," I agreed.

"So how d'ya see Mrs. Staples as the perp?"

I shook my head. "She was in Syracuse with her mother the day of the murder. The alibi's been verified by the mother, but duplicity is the hallmark of this particular family, so you might want to get third-party verification."

Provost looked at me admiringly. "You know what I don't get? I don't get how you can use so many words and not run out."

I was completely nonplussed.

Provost smiled slightly. Then he looked at his notepad. "Okay. Next is the jealous husband. I checked on that class he said he was at. He wasn't there for most of it."

I shifted in my seat. "Neville," I finally admitted, "does not have a verifiable alibi. But Luisa swears he didn't know with whom she was involved until you let the cat out of the bag, which, of course, was sometime after the crime was committed." I deliberated. "To be frank with you, Simon, if Neville had done it, it would appeal enormously to this woman's vanity. I do not trust her as a witness. Which is why I trust her initial statement that she kept Neville in the dark. If we are assessing probabilities here, I would place Neville's probable guilt at a very low number."

"You don't think he did it," Simon said, with an air of not having heard one word in ten.

"I do not."

"And what about the missus?"

I frowned. Not at the thought of Luisa's guilt, which was pleasing, but at the locution. "I doubt it. She says she was waiting for Staples at the apartment in Ithaca the morning of the murder. She spent the time pouring out her troubles to a sympathetic neighbor. That is easily verified. Not to mention the fact," I added with some distaste, "that she is a shrieker and a hysteric. There would have been a noisy altercation in the milk room. Ashley would have heard them."

"Which brings us back to the Caprettis and their kin."

"Doucetta has the volatility to commit the murder. Anyone who has a stake in the inheritance would have a substantial revenge motive. If the bad samples kept turning up, there's no question the dairy's reputation would suffer. You know how hysterical the public at large becomes over food contamination issues. A leak to the press about what is essentially pus in the milk would create a firestorm of dismay."

"Pus," Provost said with a revolted air.

"That's a fair approximation of how a reporter might look at it."

"So we've got Marietta, the granddaughter. Caterina and the husband, Frank." He tapped his pencil on his yellow pad. "I know

Frank Celestine. He bowls on the same nights I do."

"I haven't met him. Does he have the nous to commit murder?"

"If I knew what you just said I could tell you. What he is, is a blowhard and a bully. And that construction company of his is a joke." He wrote on the yellow pad, then said, "Now we come to my favorite."

"Brian Folk."

"According to Mrs. Staples, Folk and Mel were thick as thieves."

"And may have *been* thieves, from what we already know."

Provost nodded. "Right. So he and Mel have a falling-out. He follows him to the dairy 'cause he's there to take another flippin' sample. And whack, Mel ends up face-first in drink."

"Which leaves the dairy out of it altogether."

"Right."

"But what about the elevated MSCC?" I protested.

"You said the two things are separate."

"I said they *appear* to be separate," I corrected him. "I also said I *believe* them to be connected."

"I tell you a couple of rules about murder, Doc. I call it the School of the Blindingly

Obvious. Which is basically, the simplest answer's the right one. If it's staring you right in the face, you'd be an idiot to look any farther."

"Fair enough, as far as it goes," I said. "So you believe that next step is to rule out Brian Folk?"

"Seems a good place to start. I'll get Patty to do a record search in the morning, see if there are any felonies in his background. And then I'll tackle the little SOB himself."

I rose somewhat stiffly from my chair. "Madeline has signed up for the cheese-making seminar at the dairy. Her first class is tomorrow. I thought I might look in on it with her. The cheese maker is Caterina Celestine, whom I have not met. But I have an uneasy feeling about the place. Something odd is going on. And I believe Folk has nothing to do with it."

I returned home through the deepening twilight. I hadn't seen my wife or my dog since breakfast. The hot dog I'd eaten had proven a most unsatisfactory lunch. I had missed my late afternoon drink on our porch, where Madeline and I discussed the events of the day. There was an ache in my joints that was becoming all too familiar. The hours-long trek through the pastures that afternoon had brought muscles into play that had been unused for some years.

Therefore, I was in no mood to see Victor Bergland sitting at my kitchen table next to my wife.

"Hello, sweetie," Madeline said. "Look who's here!" She rose and greeted me with a kiss. She smelled faintly of chlorine from her swim. Lincoln came and leaned against my knees, a habit of his when he is feeling neglected.

"Hello, Victor."

"Hello, Austin."

"I see Madeline has supplied you with some of my Scotch?"

"Actually," Madeline said, handing me a glass of that selfsame nectar, "Victor brought some."

I took a sip. It was single malt. A Laphroaig, in fact. I took another. I began to feel quite mellow.

Madeline kissed me again. "Sit down, sweetie. Joe said you stopped off to see Simon. Did the two of you get anything to eat? No? You just wait right there."

She bustled off to the kitchen. I sat across from Victor. He didn't look like himself. Lincoln put his paw on my knee in an imperative way. I stroked my dog's ears and tried to decide what was odd about my old friend. "You're wearing a shirt with a reptile

168

on the pocket."

Madeline set a plate of cold potato salad, strawberries, and southern smoked ham in front of me. "It's a Lacoste," she said cheerfully.

I knew the name. "It's what they call a golfing shirt," I said. "Have you taken up golfing, Victor?"

He looked down at himself. Victor has a bit of a belly. The knit made him look as if he swallowed a basketball. "Thelma thinks it'd be a good activity for my retirement."

I stopped cold, a forkful of ham in midair. "Your retirement?"

Madeline bustled back to the table. She bustles when she's flummoxed — a rare occurrence with my self-possessed wife. "Yes," she said brightly. "Now that Thelma and Victor have less need for his salary as a professor, she's thinking maybe they should golf. And go on a cruise or two. And not work."

"We've just joined the Summersville Country Club," Victor said. "The course is by some fellow who's top-notch. Robert Trent Jones, that's it."

"The Summersville Country Club is filled with Republicans, Victor."

Madeline went tsk. "There's nothing wrong with Republicans, sweetie. Some of our best friends are Republicans."

"I don't think so," I said testily.

"Joe's a Republican," Madeline said.

I set my empty glass on the table. Madeline filled it up again. I kept my gaze on Victor. "You're thinking of resigning your position as chair?"

"Thelma thinks it's taking too much time. And what am I contributing to veterinary science anyway? I haven't done any real research in years. I spend all my time on committees, trying to keep everybody happy, which is just about impossible in a university atmosphere, as you well recall."

I thought of the relish with which Victor entered the lists of engagement. It would not be too far-fetched to say that academic politics were his aphrodisiac. Nothing put a sparkle in his eye or a spring in his step like disaffected associate professors squabbling over who should be teaching remedial chemistry. (Kindergarten classes were oases of reason compared to the rationales offered by those that flatly refused to teach them.)

"And now that Thelma's come into this inheritance, she'd like us to spend more time together. Which," he added in an overly hearty tone, "I would like to do, of course."

I looked helplessly at my wife. It was clear that Victor had come to us for assistance.

Of what type, I couldn't imagine. She sat down next to Victor and took his hand warmly in her own.

"Don't you even think about quittin' the university. Thelma needs something important to do with her life, Victor. And the two of you just got a pot load of something that'll let her do it.

"She's going to become Summersville's best-known cheese maker."

EIGHT

"I just couldn't see any way to nose around the Caprettis' business unless we had a logical reason to ask all the questions," Madeline said. "Mrs. Capretti's not the most sociable soul, apparently, but from what they tell me down at the Embassy, she's a real sharp businesswoman. If Thelma walks up to her and says she's thinking about opening a cheese shop, and she's going to want to sell Tre Sorelle cheeses in it, Mrs. Capretti's got to pay her some mind."

It was Tuesday morning. We were on Route 96, headed toward the dairy and the first of Madeline's cheese-making classes. The clinic was in Joe and Allegra's capable hands. I was to meet Leslie Chou at the dairy and we planned to finish up the QMPS and take a repeat set of random samples of milk from the doe herd and the milk line.

"Thelma needs something to take her

mind off punishing poor Victor for that little lapse he had last month. Startin' her own business will be just the ticket. I think I had a pretty good idea, if I do say so myself. We're going to kill two birds with one stone. Get the inside skinny on who wants to mess up that perfectly nice dairy, and give Thelma an interest in life other than tormentin' her husband."

The little lapse in question was an affair with one of his students.

"Do you think that's why Thelma is demanding Victor quit his job and start golfing?" I said. "To punish him? I find that very hard to believe." And quite excessive, I thought. All the poor fellow did was have an affair. He had apologized most abjectly.

Madeline's face is quite expressive. "Austin, you just don't understand women!"

"But . . . Thelma? Cheese making?"

"You probably forgot all about this, Austin, but the woman majored in home ec at Cornell thirty-five years ago when the school offered such a thing. And she minored in accounting."

"Thelma?"

"Thelma."

I drove along in silence. The pink stucco buildings of the dairy appeared in the distance. "Have you discussed this with her?"

Madeline smiled the smile that makes two dimples in her cheeks. "Not directly. But you heard what I told Victor last night. You two just shut up and leave it to me."

I pulled into the dairy's drive, and parked where the sign indicated I should. Thelma's Hummer was already there. It had attracted the admiring attention of the dairy workers, Ashley Swinford among them. Ashley raised her hand in greeting and trotted over to say hello. "Hi, Dr. McKenzie. Hi, Mrs. Mc-Kenzie. How's Sunny doing?"

"She's lost a good fifty pounds," I said, "and she's due to lose at least seventy-five more. I am happy to say she's much improved. Allegra has her under light excerise. She may be ready to come home sooner than I'd thought."

Ashley fell in step beside us as we proceeded along the path to the creamery. "That's great. I miss her. I talked to Ally yesterday and I'm going over to ride at Mrs. Gernsback's this afternoon after I get off work. I think she wants what I know about Mel's murder. I mean, she's part of your detective agency, isn't she?"

"If you know anything germane about the murder, you should tell the police," I said. "But yes, she does want to talk with you. At my request, she's going to ask you for some background on the people in the dairy."

"Really?" We stopped at the entrance to the creamery. The door was open to a large room with a concrete floor. Long stainless-steel tables were set around the walls. The center of the room held workstations with sinks in the middle and counter space on either side. There were seven or eight people in the room, Thelma among them. "I don't know if I can help," Ashley said dubiously. "But I'll try. You know it's weird. I didn't, like, feel all that much after I found Mel upside down in the bulk tank? I was, like, totally cool with it? But last night . . ." She stopped and rubbed her bare arms, as if struck by a chill. "I had the most awful dreams."

"Murder is awful," Madeline said. "You get any more of those dreams, you'll want to talk to your mother about it."

"It's not," Ashley said, as if struck by an amazing thought, "like you see it on TV."

Murder is not like you see it on TV.

But the cheese-making class was exactly like those cooking shows that one *does* see on TV, complete with a perky chef in the person of Caterina Celestine, Doucetta's eldest daughter. She had been a lovely woman in her youth. But age — or perhaps her notorious husband — had put lines of strain around her mouth and eyes and dusted her hair with gray. She wore an apron with the brightly colored Tre Sorelle logo. Her hair was pulled back under an unattractive plastic cap, a necessity in food preparation in these heavily legislated times, but when she smiled, you saw the woman she had been.

In the course of my study of cattle, I had of course learned the basics of cheese making. But the knowledge was forty years out of date, and I remained in the class, curious to see if time had made a difference in technique.

It had not. There are over five hundred types of cheese, and it is all created the same way. Cheese is curdled milk drained of whey. Milk is heated to a temperature suitable to activate the bacteria in the enzyme rennet and then curdled with the rennet, which can be derived from animal or vegetable sources. A starter culture is added to the mixture. The cheese may be pressed or merely molded. It is then aged in a cool environment until the cheese maker decides it is worthy of consumption. There are many variables in cheese making, and the deliciousness of the product depends on the skill of the preparer. The freshness and clarity of the milk, the dirt of the animals, the variety of rennet, and the strain of starter culture are just a few of the variables. Even the temperature and humidity of the room and the type of equipment can affect the end result.

The room was open to the outside air — refreshing on this pleasant August day. And the equipment was of the finest stainless steel and the best quality plastic. I counted eight students, excluding Madeline and Thelma, and the population was just as varied as the cheeses Caterina displayed to the class. There was a couple who could be from nowhere other than New York. A lawyer and a stockbroker, from the gist of their somewhat acrimonious conversation. There was a family with a cheerful blonde wife and mother accompanied by two talkative boys and a bored-looking husband. Looking quite out of place were two young men in sunglasses, older than Joe by some years, dressed in identical rumpled linen suits and dark T-shirts. Caterina cast the two a somewhat nervous glance, and then welcomed the class to the dairy.

She proposed to make Feta cheese. It takes about ten pounds of milk to make a pound of cheese, so she began with a twenty-gallon supply of raw goat's milk. Unlike cheddars, Goudas, and the infinitely more complicated blue cheeses, Feta comes from a simple recipe and doesn't need to be ripened at a controlled temperature. It is ideal for the beginner, since it merely requires brining in a 14 percent solution before it is edible.

I watched for a few moments, and then mindful of my task as a Quality Milk Production Services team member, I went to search for Leslie Chou.

I found her in the milk room. She stood looking down into the four-hundred-gallon bulk tank, staring at the body of Brian Folk, Summersville's latest tax assessor.

"It is just a cryin' shame that these young girls have to find the bodies," Madeline said in a fierce whisper. She sat next to Leslie on the front steps to the dairy office. Her arm was around the poor girl, who didn't seem to realize she was crying.

"Leslie, what was it that brought you into the milk room?" I asked.

"I don't know that now's a good time to ask questions, Austin."

"It's okay, Mrs. McKenzie." Tears poured down Leslie's face, misting her spectacles. She removed them, cleaned them with a tissue Madeline took from her capacious purse, and put them back on again. She blinked at me and sniffed, still crying away like a little spigot. It was most distressing. "I was looking for you, Professor. I'd collected twenty samples from the does still waiting to be milked. You said to go ahead without you, right?"

"I did, indeed," I said in a somewhat overhearty way. I am never sure what to do when women cry. I took a tissue from Madeline and polished my own spectacles. "All labeled and stored correctly, I assume?"

"Yes, sir." The tears ebbed from a torrent to a trickle. "I put them in a metal case and locked it. Nobody touched those samples but me."

"Very good. Very wise." I cleared my throat. Simon and the full panoply of scene-of-the-crime people, med techs, and policemen would be here within minutes. I'd closed and locked both doors to the milk room. Thelma stood guard at the milking parlor end, and Madeline and I stood guard at the other. No one could get into the room without passing through the office. And to pass through the office, one had to pass through us. "And so you took a shortcut through the milk room?"

She took a deep breath. "Not exactly. I guess I'm like any other rubbernecker. I wanted to see where Melvin Stap . . ." She bit her lip.

"Take a deep breath, sweetie," Madeline said.

Leslie leaned into Madeline's soft bosom. "Anyhow. I was curious. I lifted the lid and looked in and there he was."

The tears were suddenly replaced by shaking.

"All right, now, Leslie," Madeline said. "We're goin' to go sit in the car so you can put your head back and not think about this for a bit." She cast a beseeching glance at me. "You suppose Simon would pitch a fit if I just took her along home?"

I hesitated.

"Honest," Leslie said, "I don't know how come I'm acting like this. I'm fine, really."

Ashley emerged from the small crowd of people who had gathered in the driveway. It was composed of the family and New York couple from the cheese-making class and four of the dairy workers. The two men in sunglasses had disappeared. And there was no sign of Caterina. "Hey, Leslie," Ashley said soberly. "You okay?"

"Sure." This was delivered between chattering teeth.

"That's, like, how I felt last night when I thought about finding Mel," Ashley said. "I got up and drank some hot tea. You want to come with me and see if I can make you some hot tea? There's a kettle and stuff in the store."

"You found one, too," Leslie said.

"Yeah." Ashley paused. "It was, like, totally gross."

Leslie hiccupped and smiled. "Tea'd be good."

Ashley looked at Madeline and me. "Is that okay?"

"I think it'd be good for both of you," Madeline said firmly. She looked up, as we all did, at the sound of sirens careening down Route 96. "You stay in the store, mind. The lieutenant is going to want to talk to you after a bit."

Kevin Kiddermeister pulled up with a screech of tires. He shut off the police siren, but left the red lights flashing. The ambulance was right behind him. The siren died with a wail, and the EMTs jumped out of the cab. Behind both vehicles, at a slower pace, came Simon in his old Ford Escort.

"Tell me it's not Brian Folk," he said, as he got out of the car. He jerked his head at Kevin, who began setting up yellow police tape. The young patrolwoman with him went to the crowd of onlookers and started taking names and addresses.

"I would love to be able to tell you it isn't.

But it certainly appears to be."

"Dead?"

"Very. And not recently."

Provost shook his head and made a disgusted noise. "Damn! I should have talked to the SOB last night. We'd better see what we got here."

Madeline touched my arm. "I'm going to find Thelma."

I nodded.

I followed Simon into the office, and from there to the milk room itself. We paused just inside the door. The EMTs pushed past us and went straight to the body.

"Try not to touch anything but the poor soul himself," Simon said.

No more than a cursory examination was needed. Folk had been dead for some hours. And he had not died in the bulk tank. It had taken me no more than a moment to see that full rigor mortis had set in — which meant the time of death had been between eight to ten hours before Leslie's discovery. And both knees had been broken to make the body accommodate the size of the bulk tank. So he had not been hit over the head and drowned, as Staples had.

Someone was sending a message. To whom and about what was yet to be determined.

The forensics team was next to arrive. Simon watched them at work, his eyes flicking back and forth from the tank to the room itself. After a bit, he gestured to me. "Not much more I can do here. You saw what I saw, I take it?"

"The time of death was at least eight hours ago, if not more. This hot weather may have retarded the onset of rigor if the body had lain outside for any length of time. And he was killed elsewhere and brought here fairly recently." I looked at my watch. "Within the last hour, I should think."

Provost eyed me narrowly. "And why is that?"

"You noticed the milk spilled on the floor? If the body had been in the tank while the milking was going on, the automatic shutoff valve would have kicked in before the normal amount of milk was piped into the tank. A body that size will displace at least a hundred gallons. Someone would have come in to check why the valve kicked in. Milking ended about half an hour ago. Therefore, the body was placed in the tank between nine thirty and ten."

I sat on the steps with Madeline and Leslie as soon as I realized how close I was to actually discovering the murderer. With one exception, no one had exited the dairy since

I found the body. When I found Leslie, I took her outside and called Madeline on my cell phone. It was a matter of five minutes — less — when the courtyard wasn't under observation.

"Somebody could have slipped out in that five minutes," Simon objected. "Or before Leslie came into the milk room. And what's this exception?"

"No question about that at all. The perpetrator must have left on foot or by vehicle. However, the parking lot has the same number of cars in it since I arrived. I would have heard a tractor or a truck from the cheese-making room. And how could a person on foot hide, Simon?" I gestured around me. The dairy was set high on a hill to take advantage of the view of Cayuga Lake. One could see a mile in all directions. "I suggest you could check and see if anyone's hiding in the goat pens or on the farm grounds. Whoever did this has to be close by. And there is one other thing. The cheese-making class began at nine o'clock. Two young men joined us. They never left the site, but when I emerged from the dairy office, they had gone. The milking was still going on when Madeline and I arrived here at about eight forty-five. They were in front of me from that time until just after the body was discovered. They were roughly five-ten, about 160 pounds, dressed in white linen suits and dark T-shirts. Black hair, sunglasses, and swarthy complexions."

"They both looked alike?"

"They could have been brothers." As, in fact, I surmised they were. But I decided to keep that conjecture to myself for the moment.

Simon nodded. He spoke into his cell phone. A few moments later, the patrol people started a search of the barns. And in the far distance, the village fire alarm sounded. A search by the volunteer firemen of Summersville would be thorough.

"There is one other place the murderer could be, of course." I pointed up the hill to the house. "It's odd, isn't it? There isn't one member of the Capretti family out here to see what's going on."

Simon stared at me a moment. Then he said, "Let's go."

We walked up the steps to the ornate front door. Simon's face was a study in frustration. "I'm undermanned here, Doc." He turned and looked down the path to the scene below. "I think you're right. I think whoever did this is hiding out nearby and it's driving me absolutely crazy."

"We can only make the best with what we

have." I raised my hand to the door. "Shall I knock?"

But before I could do so, the door swung open. Marietta Capretti smiled at us. She was dressed in jeans, sandals, and a skimpy T-shirt that showed her smooth skin when she gestured us in. I heard Simon sigh heavily.

"We're all in the dining room," she said. "My auntie Caterina's response to World War Three will be a sour cream coffee cake." We accompanied her into a spacious dining room. The view out the French doors to the lake was spectacular. The walls were sepia shading to cream. A wrought-iron chandelier hung over a long, black oak refrectory table. And around the table sat Caterina, a discontented-looking man in a Celestine Builders T-shirt with the name Frank embroidered on the pocket, Doucetta herself, and the two young men in white linen.

"Those the guys?" Simon said. His hand went to where his shoulder holster would be if he wore a gun, which he didn't. He dropped his hand and advanced on the two men.

I spoke up. "These, I believe are the Celestine brothers."

"My grandsons," Doucetta said proudly. "They arrived last night. The curse has been lifted!"

Simon looked at me, bewildered.

"Grandmamma thinks the place has been cursed since Tony and Pietro left for Siena," Marietta said. She sat down at the table. "Now they're back."

"And the milk will pass your crummy tests," Doucetta said. She had a large cup of espresso in front of her. She slurped it noisily. "The milk will pass your crummy tests because *they*" — she pointed a long, skinny finger at Pietro and Tony — "found out what was poisoning my milk!"

"You did?" I said.

One of the brothers was slightly shorter than the other. He took off his dark glasses and looked at me blandly. "You're this doc *Donna* Doucetta's been talking about?"

"I am."

"Well, you should have looked at the pipes, my friend. There was a fresh patch of stucco along the path of the pipe from the milking parlor to the tank. Tony and me, we chipped away at it, and guess what?"

"I don't guess," I said.

He pulled a wine spigot from his pocket. It was the type that plugs onto an open bottle of wine and allows you to pour. "Stuck right into the pipe. Some creep's been pumping crap into the milk."

I took the spigot and examined it. "Quite an ingenious saboteur," I remarked.

Tony looked pleased. I handed the gizmo back to Pietro.

Doucetta struck the table with the palm of her hand. "So! You see! My boys here found out what you smarty pants could not! My milk will pass any test you arseholes throw at it."

"As long as there are no more bodies in your bulk tanks," I said rather pointedly.

An absolute silence fell over the table. Caterina broke it. "Can I get you both some coffee?" she asked nervously. "Maybe a piece of coffee cake?"

"For cripes' sake, Caterina," Frank said. "Shut it, will you?"

Marietta gave her uncle a glance of dislike. "I imagine that the lieutenant and Dr. McKenzie would welcome a cup of coffee, Auntie. Do you need a hand?"

"No, no, dear. You sit there. I'll be back in a minute." She rustled away to the kitchen. Simon sat at the head of the table, without invitation. I sat down next to him. "Fine," he said. "I've got a couple of questions for you all."

He looked at the Celestine brothers. "You two got your passports on you?"

Pietro half rose from the chair and pulled

his wallet from his rear pants pocket. He tossed two green passport books at the lieutenant. Simon opened them and read them carefully. "You're Italian citizens?"

Pietro nodded.

"And you left Italy the sixth of August of this year." He looked up. "Yesterday, in fact."

"I picked them up at the airport last night," Caterina said. She came with a tray, a carafe, and two cups of coffee. She placed the filled cups before us and refilled everyone else's. It was quite strong and as good as the coffee from our local supplier, Gimmie!

Simon looked at me, and I could almost read his mind. Arresting outsiders for the murders would have been an easy, politic solution for him. Summersville was a small town. Violent crime was almost unknown to us. It would be a comfort, locally, if no one we knew was involved. But the arrival dates cleared them of the Staples murder, and my own observation of the brothers seemed to put them in the clear for the death of Brian Folk. "Well, welcome back to America," he said easily. He spun the passports down the table. Pietro nodded gravely and stowed them carefully in his breast pocket.

Provost addressed everyone else. "About

ten fifteen this morning, Leslie Chou discovered the body of the Summersville tax assessor at the dairy."

Doucetta said, "Bullshit." Since the news of the murder appeared to surprise nobody, I assumed this was a comment on the general tenor of the day.

"Four days ago, Ashley Swinford found another guy in the same place. Also dead. Also an inspector. Seems like you folks have got some kind of pattern going." Provost had a steely gaze that he used to good effect. He swept the table, looking keenly at each person in turn, and said, "I want to know which one of you discovered the body before Miss Chou."

Nobody spoke. But the brothers glanced at Frank and looked away. There are no flies of any kind on Simon. He homed in on Celestine like a red-tailed hawk after a pigeon. "You, sir," he said. "I'd like an account of your movements this morning."

"Tell him, Frank," Marietta said. "Or one of us will."

Celestine moved uneasily.

"Were you near the milk room between nine thirty and ten o'clock?" Provost demanded.

Celestine picked at his lower lip. He looked at his mother-in-law. "Do I need a lawyer?"

"You need a slap up the side of the head."

Provost leaned forward. "Did you kill Brian Folk?" His voice was a growl.

"See!" Frank burst out. "I told you they'd think that. Goddammit, anyhow. *No!* No, I did not kill that sack of sh—"

"Shut up, you!" Doucetta said. Then, rather primly, she added, "I do not put up with this kind of language where we eat."

This made no sense, but I let it pass. But I couldn't let Frank Celestine's behavior pass. "You put the body in the bulk tank," I said.

Frank turned on his wife, "You stupid cow! This coffee's cold!"

Pietro got up from his chair, sauntered around to the end of the table, and bent down and whispered in his father's ear. Celestine paled. He muttered "sorry" at his wife. Pietro sat down again.

"Did you?" Provost asked. "Did you put Brian Folk's body in the tank?"

Celestine attempted a laugh. The sound was between a snarl and a choke. Most unattractive. "Seemed like a good idea at the time. I thought it'd be a pretty good joke, finding it where that jerkola Staples bought the farm." He began to talk faster and faster. "I was out for a walk after

191

breakfast. It was too early to go down to this . . . meet this guy I'm supposed to see about a big job over in Syracuse. So I went out. For a walk. And I went down the lane behind the kidding barn and there he was. Flat on his face in the compost pile. I checked him out, and he was dead, all right. Flies crawling around his eyeballs and already beginning to smell a little bit. There's a wheelbarrow that we keep right there so I wrestled him into it. Had to whack his legs with a hammer to make him fit." He flexed his right arm in an absent-minded way. The man was disgusting, but he was in excellent shape. "And I thought it'd be funny if he ended up where the other one ended up."

"And then," Marietta said tiredly, "he came and told me what he'd done. By that time, that poor little Chinese girl was sitting on the front steps crying all over Mrs. McKenzie. So I got on the cell phone and got Auntie Caterina and my cousins up here." She shrugged. "We waited for you. I knew you'd figure out Frank had moved the body sooner or later. I mean" — she waved her hand in the air — "forensics, right?"

This was a positive effect of all those highly dramatized crime shows on television. It is unlikely that our forensics team would have discovered any evidence positively linking Frank to the mere removal of the body. However, it was very likely that the team would discover any evidence linking Frank to the murder. I looked at Marietta with renewed respect. She was covering all the bases. She was both beautiful and clever.

"Fine," Provost said. He got to his feet. Simon wears a sports coat for any number of reasons, the chief being that it is a useful way to hide what he carries on his belt. He unsnapped a pair of handcuffs and advanced on Celestine. "You're coming with me, sir."

"But I didn't kill him!" Frank shouted. "All I did was move him a few hundred feet farther from where I found him. It was supposed to be a joke!"

"You unlawfully moved a body." Simon snapped the cuffs on. "And that's enough for me. We'll continue the rest of this conversation down at the station." He looked over at me, "So how'd you know he did it, Doc?"

"There's compost in the cuffs of his chinos. There was compost floating in the bulk tank. It seemed like a logical conclusion."

"So we dump more milk!" Doucetta shouted. "Arsehole!"

NINE

"Goat pate," Thelma said. "Goat sausage. That's the way to increase the market share." She turned to Deirdre, who had just placed Monrovian Specials in front of all four of us. "Maybe even goat hamburger. What do you think?"

"You'll have to talk to Rudy about that," Deirdre said diplomatically. "You guys all set? Dr. Bergland? Maddy?"

She did not address me. I was not all set. My Monrovian Special was sadly free of beer-battered onion rings and the garlic-butter-saturated toasted bun. If we were to eat at the Embassy twice within a week, Madeline decreed, I would have to forgo the major sources of cholesterol. Any protest I would have made was rendered nugatory by the fact that Madeline and Deirdre were in cahoots; Deirdre saw to it that I didn't get onion rings more than once a week whether Madeline was standing guard or not. I shook catsup liberally over the burger and made do with fresh onion, tomato, and lettuce.

"The cheese-making class was fascinating," Thelma said. In some way I couldn't fathom, she was beginning to look more like the old Thelma. "I'm so glad I decided to get a look in, as they say. Thank goodness Caterina had finished by the time that body was discovered. And wasn't it lucky that the police put us all in the retail shop while we waited to be interviewed? All in all, it was a very interesting day."

I raised my eyebrows and glanced at Madeline, who smiled mysteriously. Provost had insisted we leave the investigation to him. So it seemed wise to go to the Embassy for lunch.

Thelma rapped her knuckles on the tabletop. "Victor? I am seriously thinking of going into business." In an absentminded way, she removed three of her clanking gold bracelets and dropped them into her purse. I realized she had forgone the glittery blue stuff on her eyelids.

"What kind of business?" Victor asked.

"A cheese shop," she said. "But not just any cheese shop. A gourmet cheese shop."

"Thelma went through the Tre Sorelle tasting rooms while we were waiting for the police to let us all go," Madeline said. "She was charmed. I was, too. It's gorgeous. There's all kinds of cute stuff in there."

"Doucetta is missing a number of retail opportunities," Thelma said in a grand way. "All that tat. She could be making a much bigger profit margin on higher-end goods."

"Tat?" Victor said.

"Tea cozies with a cheese motif. Mechanical mice. Rubber cheese bathtub toys."

"Those were for the kids, I suppose," Madeline said.

"My shop will be for discriminating adults. Fine wines. Fine foods. Fine cheeses. There are a lot of ways I can make this shop stand out from the crowd, and I don't need rubber bath toys to do it. Goat meat pate, for example. Caterina said they were experimenting with a few recipes, but I'll bet you I can go her one better. You remember, Victor, that I have a degree in home economics." She removed another bangle. "Madeline, I'm thinking of scouting locations this afternoon. Would you care to come with me?"

"Scouting locations?" Victor said. "Goat meat pate?" He looked somewhat bewildered. I can't say that I blamed him. News of Brian Folk's murder had hit the local radio show within an hour of the event.

Filled with husbandly concern, Victor had called, and agreed to meet us for lunch. He had left a house crammed with brochures on yachts Thelma wanted to buy and expensive vacations she wanted to take. Now she was talking about *making* money. "Locations for a gourmet cheese shop? In Summersville?"

"A far better use of my inheritance than golf club memberships and yachts," Thelma said reprovingly. "Really, Victor. You can be awfully frivolous at times."

Victor opened his mouth to protest and said, "Ouch!" instead. I presume Madeline had kicked him under the table. Then he said humbly, "Will you want me to work in this cheese shop?"

"Victor! You have a position at the university to maintain."

"But you said . . . Ouch! Madeline, cut that out! Okay. Fine, great. You pick a good spot for this store, Thelma. It's a terrific idea. Absolutely terrific." With every appearance of a man confused and buffeted by a kindly fate, he beamed and bit into his hamburger.

Thelma took a pen from her purse and began scribbling on a napkin. "Furnishings. Store facility. Permits. There's just a ton of stuff to do here. Madeline, if you like, you may give any help I might need."

"I'd love to, sweetie," Madeline said promptly. "I think the best thing I can do for you is talk to the people at Tre Sorelle. I'll bet Mrs. Capretti herself would be more than willin' to tell me how much stuff costs, and what kind of investment you're looking at here."

"Business plan," Thelma muttered, scribbling away.

Madeline shot a mischievous glance at me. "I'm hopin' she'll give us the name of her accountants. I'll bet they can give us a real good idea, too."

"Ask her about this plan for the pate," Thelma ordered. "Find out who her supplier is."

"They probably use the culls from the dairy," Victor said through a mouthful of onion rings.

"I doubt that," I said. "There is a world of difference between the dairy and meat breeds. You should be looking at a Boer goat supplier, Thelma. Such as George Best."

"Two days at a goat dairy and you're an expert on caprines?" Victor said.

"It took me far less time than that to come up to speed," I said. "But I've always been quick to absorb new information."

"Right," Victor said. "Like the time it took

you to get through the genetics on double-muscled steers."

"The science took me no time at all. It was the ultimate utility of the Belgian Blue that presented a challenge. And was I right? How many Blues do you find at auction these days, Victor?"

"So you were right." He paused. "Once."

I bit into my own hamburger. It was good to have the rude and obstreperous Victor back. The four of us ate in companionable silence for a bit.

Madeline sat across from me, so that she was facing the front door. She looked over my shoulder and her eyebrows went up. "Well, now," she said. "I've heard that if you wait long enough, practically everyone in town comes into the Embassy, and look who just did."

I turned. Gordy Rassmussen had just walked in. He stopped for a moment to let his eyes adjust from the bright August day outside, then headed straight for the bar and grabbed a stool.

"*Who* just came in?" Thelma demanded.

"You can see for yourself," Victor said.

"Just tell me, Victor. Is that too much to ask?" She sat next to me, and would have had to turn around to find out. Apparently, it was much easier to ask Victor. Married life was indeed back to normal for them. I felt quite happy about it.

"The town supervisor, Gordy Rassmussen," Victor said. "He's the guy that hired Brian Folk, isn't he?" He laughed unsympathetically. "If he's hiding out, he's picked the wrong place to do it."

"He's probably just here to eat his lunch," Madeline said. She craned her neck. "Although that's his second beer in as many seconds."

"Excuse me," I said. "I need to spend just a few minutes with Gordon."

"Hello, Doc," he said glumly as I approached the bar. "Sit down and have a cold one."

"It's a bit early in the day, thank you." I settled onto a stool. "Although I will have a cup of coffee, Deirdre."

"Heard you were out to the dairy this morning," Gordy said. He was a big, rubicund fellow with the remnants of blond hair in a fringe around his scalp. His usually jovial manner was absent.

"I was, indeed."

He consumed half of his Rolling Rock in one swig. "Rita's gonna be on me like flies on a dead raccoon."

"Ah, yes." It was an election year. In less than three month's time, Gordy's tenure as town supervisor would be either renewed or not.

"He came recommended, you know."

"Brian Folk," I said.

"I've been catching a lot of heat. Nicky Ferguson kind of fell down on the job, if you catch my drift." He tapped the beer bottle. "Couple of these, and Nicky'd kind of look the other way. Say you put one of those aboveground pools in for the grandkids. After a beer or two, Nicky didn't think that'd add much to the total tax package so he'd overlook it. This Brian Folk had a whole different attitude. You put a couple of gnomes in the front garden and, blam, you're looking at a six percent increase."

"And Folk was recommended by whom?"

"By who, Doc," he said with a kindly air, "recommended by who."

"The preposition is the object of the sentence," I said rather testily, "and the proper case is the dative."

Gordy blinked at me, as if I'd been speaking a language other than our own. "Is that a fact?"

"It is not a fact, as such; it is a rule of language. And where did you find Brian Folk?"

"He did a good job over to Covert. They were in the same kind of spot we are. The

201

assessments were way behind the increase in house prices. Brian — he didn't care who you were or how many beers you gave him — he'd up the price on the house of Jesus Christ himself. And the town needs the tax revenue, Doc. No question about it. If we want to keep our streets clear of snow, the garbage picked up, the old folks home running the right way, we got to have the budget to do it. I know people don't like it, but where will we be at if we don't wake up to the facts?"

"I voted for you in the last election, and I'll vote for you again, Rassmussen. I think you're a responsible politician, all things considered. I also think you're ducking my question. Who urged Folk on you?"

"It was that one up at the dairy."

"Tre Sorelle? The goat dairy?"

"Yeah. Frank Celestine."

I excused myself from the rest of lunch and hastened down to Provost's office. He was in. And he was very interested in what I had to tell him.

The police station in Summersville has one cell. It is carpeted and it has a television. Its floor-to-ceiling bars face Provost's office. Simon and I walked across the hall to the cell and looked in. Celestine stared sullenly back.

"For heaven's sake, why?" I said. "Why did you urge Rassmussen to hire a tax assessor who would up the appraisal on your own mother-in-law? And why did Gordy follow your recommendation?" (What remained unspoken was why *anyone* would follow up on a recommendation made by Frank Celestine. The man was a notorious slacker.)

"I imagine there was a little quid pro quo, as far as Gordy was concerned." Simon scratched the back of his head. "You offer to pave Gordy's driveway, Celestine? Or maybe give the village a good price on fixing up the high school auditorium?"

"It was just a freakin' bit of business," Celestine said. "And yeah, I lowballed the estimate on the high school." He snickered. "Or at least Gordy thought I did. Made him look good to the board." He had a high, unpleasant giggle and an annoying propensity to use it. "You should have seen Doucetta's face when the assessment came in the mail. I was keeping an eye out for it, you know. Delivered it to her myself."

"And it was just to annoy your mother-in-law?"

"Why not? She's spent the last forty years annoying the heck out of me. No skin off my nose if the assessment goes up. Only person I know had the guts to face up to the old bat was Brian." Frank sucked his teeth reflectively. "Had a lot of guts, Brian did."

Simon shook his head in disgust. The two of us went back into his office and sat in our usual spots: Simon behind his desk, and I in the one comfortable chair.

"Good heavens," I said. "Do you suppose we've discovered the murderer that easily?"

"Wouldn't that be nice and tidy. But no, Celestine's alibi for the Folk murder is airtight."

"Surely not."

"Surely is. Last night, he was at the golf club bar until one, when it closed. He was soused to the gills, so the bartender dropped him off at Doucetta's house about one thirty. The old lady came to the door herself. She got Celestine onto the couch in the living room and he passed right out. If Jim Airy's right about how much booze the guy had, there's no way he could have snuck out of the house and clocked Folk over the head. Just as a precaution, I got Liz Snyder over at the clinic to draw a blood sample to check Celestine's resting alcohol rate. It's been less than twenty-four hours since he started boozing. He's probably still drunk, which explains maybe why he found dumping the body in the bulk tank to be such a laugh riot."

Alcohol remains in the system for up to thirty days. While not definitive, the resting rate would probably prove high enough to substantiate Celestine's defense even without the witnesses at the golf club.

"I suppose you're going to let him go?"

"Of course I have to let him go. I'll charge him with moving the dead body — he admitted it, after all. But if he's going to spend any time in jail, it'll have to be the judge's decision."

I smoothed my mustache. "This is proving to be a very interesting case, Provost."

"I could do with a lot less interesting and a few more suspects. Where the heck do we go from here?"

"The sabotage," I said. "That's where we go. Folk wanted the dairy to stay in business. Someone else wanted to shut it down."

"What about this alleged connection between Folk and Staples?"

"That is quite easily explained, now that we know the kind of malicious mischief Celestine has been fomenting. Do you have the forensics report?"

"Right here."

I opened the file and pointed to the data listing the contents of Staples's vehicle.

"You see the uncontaminated milk sample that was taken from the front seat. There are two sets of fingerprints on it, Mel's and someone who isn't in the system. I'll bet you a Friday night fish fry that those prints will be Folk's. Doucetta is set on grieving that assessment. If the dairy's not functioning, she'd have a fairly good stab at lowering the fair market value of the buildings. How much is a contaminated dairy worth commercially? Folk wanted Staples to send in clean samples."

"I'll be dipped," Simon said. "So. Let me get this straight. Somehow bozo over there" — he jerked his thumb in the direction of the cell — "falls in with Folk and sets him on his mother-in-law out of sheer malice."

"You've met the man. You know his reputation. Do you doubt that as a motive?"

"No. I don't doubt Celestine's motive. But you've got to convince me that Folk wanted to play for some reason." He stared up at the ceiling and, as was his habit, began to ruminate. "Let's say you do. Let's say we find out why Folk took this one step further and hooked up with Staples so that the so . . . so . . ."

"Milk somatic cell count."

"Thanks. So that it would come back normal. So this little plan to aggravate Doucetta turns out to be a little more trouble than it's worth. I dunno," Simon said suddenly. This was a pattern I had noted in him before; he tended to argue with himself out loud. "I guess it makes sense if you look at the characters involved. Folk was a single-minded little so-and-so. Took a lot of pride in sticking to his guns as an assessor. What'd Gordy say? You couldn't bribe him for love or money. And not because he was honest, but because he had to be right? I can see that he'd go that extra step to try and get Mel to fake good results." He slapped his knees with both hands. "Okay. If I have to buy this, I will." He looked at me. "So I can see the malicious mischief angle. It doesn't account for the murders. Does Folk kill Staples because he's not playing along? That makes no sense to me. That's a motive for a psycho and these guys are your garden-variety creeps, not psycho. And who killed Folk? And how come?"

"There is the second, very curious element to this case that we have heretofore ignored."

"Heretofore, huh." Provost sighed. "And that would be?"

"Sabotage. You realize it took a fairly clever, determined person to burrow into that wall and use the wine spigot to pour pus down the pipe."

"Maybe you could not talk about pus so much."

"I haven't talked about pus at all," I protested. "In any event, I have a conjecture."

I paused. After a bit, Provost drummed his fingers on his desk. "Well?"

"I think Staples and Folk just got in the way of the saboteur."

"Got in the way," Simon repeated reflectively.

"They stumbled onto a larger plot, and they were eliminated."

Provost nodded to himself. "Okay. Okay. That I can buy. So. The sabotage. Where do we start? I don't even have a logical suspect pool."

"Greed. Lust. Revenge. An unholy triumvirate. But the triumvirate holds the key to this case. And we'll begin with the remaining players. Has Doucetta annoyed her suppliers to the point of murder? We'll put them on the list." I hesitated, and then said, "We need to interview Neville, just to clear things up. And there is the Folk-Staples business connection. I have a strong feeling there may be motives there."

We drew up a list of suspects and divided it between us.

■ ■ ■ ■

"The police department has asked us to look into all possible suspects connected with the dairy," I said to the assembled members of Cases Closed, Inc. "It is absolutely essential that we know the movements of every person at Tre Sorelle on each day of each murder.

"The lieutenant and his people are digging into Folk's and Staples's backgrounds. They have the resources to do this far better than we do." I paused, diverted by a brief vision of Cases Closed, Inc., International with a global reputation and the resoures of the CIA. "For the moment, at any rate.

"Now, Folk's body was found on the seventh, but the medical evidence suggests that he was killed on the sixth. And we know that Staples was murdered where he stood, on the fourth of August. So we need charts! Data! Graphs!"

"Sort of a 'who's-where,' " Ally said.

"An excellent name for it," I said. "We'll add that to the company's permanent procedures process."

"The who's-where includes the herd manager and the barn help, doesn't it?" Joe asked.

"It most certainly does."

I was quite happy. The entire staff of Cases Closed was assembled in our living room: Joe, Allegra, Madeline, Lincoln, and myself included. We had a client, in the form of the Summersville Police Department. We had a case. Most important, we had a billing number and a place to send the invoice.

"I can handle the barn help," Allegra said. "I'm schooling Tracker with Ashley again tomorrow. She can help verify where the people who work there were during the day. She gets to work at eight and works until five. I'll stop by the dairy, first. I'll interview everyone, set up a chart, and then we can cross-check everybody's whereabouts." She looked doubtful. "I hope my Spanish is up to talking to the barn staff."

"Pietro and Tony are at least bilingual," I said. "And they may have a little Spanish, as well. Perhaps they could be of assistance. And since they've only been in the country less than twenty-four hours, they are not suspects. I suggest you enlist their support."

"And me, Austin?" Madeline said.

"If you can accompany Thelma in her meetings with anyone from Tre Sorelle, it's possible we'll come up with more data. I hope so. We're short on facts at the moment. I will interview Marietta. She seems to have a bone to pick with the whole lot of them. She was unusually forthcoming about Doucetta's tax dodges. Perhaps she could be encouraged to reveal even more."

"What about Caterina and the horrible Frank?" Allegra asked.

I exchanged glances with Madeline. "We are going to ask Victor for some help with that," I said. "He is a member of the self-same golf club that offers liquor Celestine is unable to refuse. Madeline and I will go to dinner at the club with the Berglands tomorrow night. It's something called Ladies Night. I understand that the Wednesday night dinner is Caterina's only night free from her kitchen."

"And what about me, Doc?" Joe asked.

"According to Ashley, Doucetta irked all of her suppliers in one way or another. I have a list of those who live locally." I pulled the sheet from the file and handed it over to him. "You and I will double-team. We'll interview as many as will talk to us."

"Hm," Joe said. "The Bests are on here."

"They supply meat kids for the pate and sausage. We can't let affection affect our responsibility to the case."

"They're in their eighties!"

"Doucetta Capretti is ninety-four, and she's Provost's chief suspect at the moment.

Besides," I said, descending from the lofty, "Phyllis knows all the gossip. It's an excellent place to pick up leads."

"And so is the Swinford Vineyard?" Joe said. "I can't believe anything they supply the dairy would lead to a blood feud."

"Jonathan supplies them with five cases of wine a month. And Doucetta in full spate would drive the pope to murder."

"And Dr. Tallant from the Pastures Green Clinic?" Joe's eyebrows rose.

"She must be eliminated as a suspect. We can't play favorites, even though she is a fellow veterinarian. If Doucetta hasn't paid the bill, that could be the beginning of some very poor relations indeed." I sat back and drew breath. "It's more than likely that one or all of these suppliers will be found to have reasonable alibis for the fourth and the night of the sixth. But as you know, one must approach the solution to a murder investigation in the same way that one approaches the diagnosis of a pathological condition. Collect all relevant data, assess —"

"Doc?' Ally said. "I don't mean to interrupt you, but I've to get back to the barn and take another look at Tracker's stifle. He seemed a little tender going to the left."

"And I need to get those canning jars

from the cellar, sweetie," Madeline said. "I'll be into the tomatoes pretty soon, and I'm going to need them."

Joe got up from the leather couch where he had been taking notes. "Sorry, Doc, but I'm on duty tonight and I might as well get on to the barn check."

The room began to empty. "You are all sure that you all understand the basic process of our investigatory technique?" I called after them.

There was a chorus of "yes!" as though they spoke as one.

Lincoln put his paw on my knee and cocked his head inquiringly. "It is a unique approach to detection," I said to him. "I'm thinking of submitting a paper to the *Detective Quarterly*."

Odie settled on my other knee, and they prepared to listen.

TEN

With the other members of the Cases Closed team galloping off in all directions, Joe and I set off the next morning to interview the suppliers to Doucetta's dairy. It was Wednesday, the eighth of August. Tomorrow, Melvin Staples would have been dead close to a week. We were no closer to solving the mystery of his murder. Justice demanded that we apprehend the killer, and soon.

More important, I wanted Cases Closed to get credit for bringing in the perp. I had a feeling in my bones that the murders were linked to the dairy and not to any extracurricular criminal activities by the team of Folk and Staples. Provost, I knew, was convinced that he had successfully nudged me off the track of the real killer — and out of his hair. Our team would prove him wrong!

The first potential suspects on our interview list were George and Phyllis Best, the owners and operators of Best's Boers. The farm occupies one hundred acres overlooking the lake. They live in an old double-wide trailer. The barns are held together by spit and baling twine. But the Bests have been farmers for more than fifty years and have the healthiest, happiest goats I've ever seen. They were a happy, contented couple with happy, contented goats.

"I find it really hard to believe that either one of the Bests is involved in murder," Joe said as we drove up the winding hill to their tiny farm. "First of all, they're really old. Second, they play Mr. and Mrs. Santa Claus in the Christmas parade every year, and if they ever did do anything wrong, no Summersville jury would convict them. And I can't see either one of them getting mad enough to murder anyone."

"You may be right," I said amiably.

When we pulled into the driveway of the farm, George Best was waving a twelve-gauge shotgun at a slick-looking couple in a Buick Park Avenue with New Jersey plates. We came to a stop next to the large shed that served the Bests as a kidding barn.

"Good heavens!" I said and prepared to get out of the car.

Joe grabbed my shoulder and held me

back. "Let George know we're here, first. He's a little deaf, remember? We don't want to startle him. And for God's sake, stay out of the way of that shotgun!"

Sensible advice. I rolled down the window and called out, "George! It's Austin McKenzie."

George swung the twelve-gauge around in a circle that directed the muzzle at us. Joe and I ducked below the dash.

"Dr. McKenzie!" That light, elderly voice belonged to Phyllis Best. Cautiously, I peered through the windshield. "George says he didn't know it was you." Her voice was drowned by the roar of the Park Avenue's engine. The shotgun roared. The Buick whizzed by us in a cloud of dust and gravel. Joe leaned out of the passenger window and squinted at the rear license plate. The bumper sticker read "Lakeside Real Estate." "Got it," he said and scribbled the number on the receipt book.

"You can come out now," Phyllis said cheerily. "George says, 'Good riddance to bad rubbish.'"

Joe and I emerged from the Bronco with some caution, all the same. George waved at us, and then disappeared into the depths of the double-wide, shotgun in hand. He emerged moments later, shotgun-free, and trotted down the gravel path to meet us. He dropped a handful of shotgun shells on the picnic table that sat in their small front yard, then came up and stood beside his wife.

"How nice to see you!" Phyllis beamed. "And how is Mrs. McKenzie?"

"Quite well, thank you," I responded. "And how are the Spice Girls?" I referred to the herd of Boer does that are the foundation animals for the Bests' well-bred herd.

"The summer kids are just coming on," Phyllis said. "Basil had a ten-pound buck yesterday. We named him Baby Huey." She gestured us toward the fenced pens attached to the shed. Basil, who I had treated on prior visits to the farm, greeted me with a bleat of recognition.

Although not in her first youth, Basil was an extremely good-looking doe, with the caramel brown face characteristic of the highly bred Boer and long brown ears that curled at the tip. The rest of her was white. She nursed the largest Boer buckling I've ever seen.

"Now that's a goat," Joe said in admiration.

Basil trotted to the fence, raised herself up, and whiffed hello. Baby Huey protested the sudden departure of his breakfast with a loud *blat,* leaped into the air, spun around several times, then raced as fast as he could around the fence perimeter, ears flying in the breeze created by his passage.

"Any problems?" I asked.

"A little bout of the runs with the weanlings," Phyllis said. "But nothing major. We maybe weaned that new set of kids too early."

"You added CORID to the water? And used the penicillin?"

"We did." She turned to her husband. "What? Dear? Oh. George says to thank you for those penicillin samples you sent us." She added, innocently, "It's just amazing the stuff they give doctors for free. And so good of you to send us the extra."

I avoided Joe's raised eyebrows. The Bests lived on their Social Security checks and the income from the small amount of meat they sold Doucetta. With carcasses at a dollar twenty-five a pound, and an average weight of sixty pounds, they made little enough to keep body and soul together.

"George says you probably want to know why he was shooting at those people from New Jersey."

"Er. Yes."

Phyllis sat down at the picnic table and indicated that we should, too. "They're after us and after us to buy this acreage. They didn't seem to want to take no for an answer. They've been sending us letter after letter and the last one came special delivery at ten o'clock at night, and you can imagine what George had to say about being hauled out of bed at that hour!"

In the years I had been treating the Bests' Boers, I had never heard an audible word from George Best. Neither had anyone else I knew. Either he spoke at a pitch known only to dogs and his wife, or Phyllis had exceptional extrasensory perception.

"George keeps telling these people we won't sell."

"And they keep coming back? That comes pretty close to harassment, Mrs. Best." Joe scratched Basil's forehead as he spoke. The doe looked as lovingly at him as Ashley Swinford. "Maybe you'd like us to drop a word in Lieutenant Provost's ear?"

"The police?" Phyllis wore an apron that read "We've Got Your Goat!" She fiddled nervously with the pockets. "Well, the thing is, they have this paper."

"Who has what paper?" I asked.

She sighed. "You know Louise."

"Your daughter? Yes. She's a special educa-tion teacher at the middle school, isn't she?"

"She's about to retire. She'll be sixty-five . . . anyway, we had to take out a little mortgage on the farm a while ago, and Lou cosigned for us, because the bank needed a little more security than we had, you see."

I sighed. I knew what was coming next.

"And she — what's that word, George? Assigned. Yes, she assigned the mortgage to these people. Now, we'd been making payments right along, until a few months ago when Doucetta had all that trouble and couldn't send us the meat check. So we fell behind some, and these people" — her face turned pink with indignation — "these people want all that money at once!"

"The real estate people?" Joe said, confused.

"These real estate people say they bought the land from the ones that Louise sold the mortgage to. What? Oh. George says they didn't buy the land, they bought an option."

Joe rubbed his forehead. I myself was somewhat perplexed. Except for the motive. The motive was as clear as the sky. Behind all of these shenanigans was cold, hard cash. Lakefront property was soaring in value, due in part to general inflation, but mostly due to the rise in tourism and the influx of urbanites growing grapes.

"Louise means well," Phyllis said. "She's been after us to retire for years and years. She says the farm is getting too much for us, and in a way she's right." Unconsciously, she rubbed her hands, which were bent with arthritis like the roots of a banyan tree. "But we love it."

"Let's get back to the money you're owed from the dairy," Joe said. "Mrs. Capretti is behind in her payments?"

"One hundred and thirty-five days."

I eyed Phyllis who heard 90 percent of the gossip in Tompkins County. "Is Tre Sorelle in trouble?"

Phyllis pursed her lips. "George says there are quite a few who won't do business with them. But George says it may be just that they're Eye-talian."

This was a sad fact of country life — but probably true.

"And are they behind in payments to anyone else you know?" I asked.

"It's rough times in the farming business," Phyllis said.

It is always rough times in the farming business. That's a given.

"And she's had a couple of complaints about the carcass weight." Suddenly, she blushed bright red. "George! You know I don't approve of that kind of language about anybody! This is a Christian household, if you please!"

"She's been stiffing you on the payments?"

Joe said. "How much . . ." I nudged him, and he fell silent. Talk of money embarrassed people like the Bests.

"If refusing to pay us is 'stiffing,' then she's been stiffing us," Phyllis said. "But we have faith that God will provide."

"Not likely," Joe muttered.

"George wants to know if you dropped by for any particular reason. We heard about the murders over to the dairy." She shook her snowy head. "George thinks the world is going to hell in a handbasket. It'll be the Apocalypse next, you mark my words. I mean, what kind of world is it when folks like us are suspects?" Her blue eyes, remarkably unfaded, twinkled at me. "That is why you dropped by, isn't it, Dr. McKenzie? George heard all about this detective work you're doing down to the veterans." She leaned forward and whispered in my ear, "He'll be so disappointed if you don't ask us where we were on the nights of the murders."

"August fourth and August sixth," I said. "Where *were* you on the nights of the murders?"

"Shucks. We were at bingo. Both nights. I won eleven dollars and fifty cents on the Thursday. Didn't I tell you God will provide?" Phyllis said. "That money went straight to the feed bill. Now, what if I gave you two handsome men some of my zucchini bread?"

The zucchini bread was delicious. Phyllis's baking was widely known for its excellence. It was some time before we got back on the road.

"God will provide," Joe repeated somewhat bitterly as we drove back down the winding dirt road to Route 96. "Seems like the real estate developers are the ones being provided for. And what did the Bests do to deserve a daughter like that?"

" 'O sharper than a serpent's tooth is the something something of an ungrateful child'? No, I'm glad to say Louise is no Goneril."

Joe looked blank.

"*Lear,* my boy, *King Lear.* There is more to the story than would appear. We were out there last month, as you recall, and at the time Phyllis mentioned Louise was encouraging them to them sell up and enjoy a less arduous lifestyle. I dropped in on Louise to follow up. Madeline knows her as a dedicated teacher and a fond daughter. George has been diagnosed with congestive heart failure. You saw how Phyllis suffers from arthritis. Louise has five acres and a four-bedroom house near Trumansburg. She wishes her parents to join her with as many of the Spice Girls as is practicable, the charming Basil and her chubby progeny included."

"Oh," Joe said.

"So there is no evil real estate developer with sinister designs on their property."

"I didn't think . . ."

"No. You probably didn't. But then Madeline let drop that you are a Republican. I, on the other hand, have hopes of the evil real estate developer — at least as a motive for putting the dairy out of business. The Tre Sorelle land is worth a mint to a developer, even in these recessionary times." I frowned. "It all depends on the reason for Doucetta's withholding the meat check. If it's truly due to cash problems, I may be on to something." I looked at the list in my hand. "Next is Dr. Tallant. I'll call her clinic to see where she may be found."

"Nope," said Carrie Tallant. "She owes the clinic a pile of money." Carrie's clinic assistant said she was on a call at the ASPCA, where she worked as a general veterinary one day a week. The pound is a pleasant facility, with a lot of space for the bewildering variety of animals man either maltreats or abandons. We found her in the area dedicated to reptiles. "We've had to tell her we can't come out unless she pays something on the account. So we'll get a small check. And then we'll do a bunch of work and the receivables mount up again. It's a problem, Austin. Do we let animals suffer and maybe die because we're owed a lot of money? How do we square professional ethics with that?" She shook her head in frustration. "Anyhow. It's definitely an issue. And the high somatic cell count?" She shook her head. "I couldn't find a thing wrong with the does. She told me that she was going to let the state pay for looking into it further than that. Bless the state, I say."

I inquired as to her whereabouts on the relevant nights.

"I got married," she said. She waggled her ring finger, on which she wore a plain gold band. "We went to Niagara Falls. Just got back." She petted the snake she was treating for skin mold with one forefinger. "Know anyone that wants to adopt a boa constrictor?"

I said I would make inquiries, and we left her to her snake.

"So the dairy's not doing as well as it could be," Joe mused.

"I'd rather we had some facts, as opposed

to anecdotal evidence. You notice that Carrie hasn't yet refused to go out to treat the goats. I've known more than one farmer to manage cash flow by stringing out payments."

"Creates a lot of bad feeling," Joe observed.

"Doucetta seems impervious to bad feeling. And if she's the store-your-money-under-the-mattress type, she may simply have an inclination to hang on to every penny before it's absolutely necessary to spend it. We simply don't have enough information to determine the dairy's solvency at this point."

"What about the hay and feed guys? We can check with them."

"The dairy grows its own hay. And nobody with any sense shorts the grain salesmen — they just stop delivery. Farmers pay that bill before they buy shoes for their children, much less a Mercedes for a disaffected daughter. No, I'd much prefer to talk to the accountants." I fell silent, devising ways to coax financial information from that notoriously close-mouthed group. I had an idea that would work if Madeline gave me a hand. And Thelma, although she wouldn't realize it (and if she did, would probably refuse).

"So what's next, Doc?"

"Locally the only supplier left with a possible animus is Jonathan Swinford. We'll speak with him. This time of day, we will probably find him in the vineyard itself. And I've come up with a way to discover more about the dairy's actual finances. But first we need to speak to Swinford."

We stopped first at the lavish boutique and tasting room. A Wednesday in August is prime tourist time. The tasting bar was stacked four deep with appreciative sippers. The small café area was stuffed with people drinking lattes and gulping biscotti. At the front of the long, rectangular room, a tour group gathered at the enormous windows at the grapevines in the valley below.

All the staff members wore T-shirts with the Swinford Vineyard logo and a bunch of grapes printed across the back. I stopped one young lady with a case of Swinford's famous red zinfandel under one arm and a corkscrew in the other.

"Mr. Swinford? He's at the distillery. We just got a load of juice in."

We found Jonathan Swinford at the base of a twenty-foot stainless-steel vat, writing busily on a clipboard. He was tall and thin and wore a white dress shirt rolled up at the sleeves, a well-cut pair of trousers, and expensive loafers with no socks. A sapphire-studded Rolex adorned one wrist. If he had been a prospective donor to the vet school, Victor would have put him down for he what called a huge pile of smackers. Swinford looked up as we came down the cool concrete floor, a faint look of puzzlement on his face. "I think I know you," he said with a cordial smile. "But I can't quite place . . ."

"Austin McKenzie," I said. "My assistant, Joe Turnblad."

"Of course. The horse vet. What can I do for you gentlemen? If it's about the bill for that wretched animal, you can send it on to the house."

"No, we are not here about the bill," I said with some asperity, "and I am not here in my capacity as a 'horse vet.' We have been asked to take a look into the murders at the Tre Sorelle Dairy."

He whistled. "Oh, yes. Poor Ashley found the first body. Somebody named Staples? The milk inspector? And then there was this other fellow."

"Brian Folk," I said.

He shook his head. "Sorry. I don't know him. I think I ran across Staples once when I came to pick Ash up from work. Good-looking guy. Reminded me of Mel Gibson."

His eyes narrowed. "This doesn't have anything to do with my daughter's discovery of the body, does it? She's handling it pretty well, but my wife says it was pretty traumatic for her."

"No, this doesn't involve Ashley, as such."

"As such?" he asked sharply.

"We're more interested in your relationship with Mrs. Capretti."

"Who told you I had a relationship with Ms. Capretti?" He tapped his pencil against the clipboard impatiently.

"You sell five cases of wine to the Tre Sorelle retail operation each month."

He ran his tongue around his lower lip. "We do? Let me think. I believe you're right." He smiled and placed his hand under my elbow. "Let's go into my office and see what the file says."

We followed him out of the distillery to a small office located just inside the front door of another large building. He looked over his shoulder as he unlocked the office door. "This is where we bottle. Our gallonage is about fifty thousand a year. You can see why I can't recall a five-case sale right off the top of my head." The door opened and he stepped aside. "Please come in. Would you like anything? Coffee? Or would you like to try our 2002 Chardonnay? That was our first gold medal winner, you know. I'd appreciate your opinion."

I resisted the temptation to take him up on the offer of the Chardonnay. I had indeed tasted that particular vintage, and it was excellent. "Some coffee would be welcome."

He seated himself at a rosewood desk and gestured toward two comfortable chairs placed around a small, round conference table. He pressed an intercom button, requested coffee, and then pulled the keyboard to his computer forward. "Tre Sorelle, you said?" He tapped away. "Yes, we send five cases a month to them from May until late September. We don't sell much locally in the down season."

"But you ship all over the world," I said.

"Oh, yes, where the export taxes don't make it prohibitive."

"Does Tre Sorelle pay you on time?"

He tapped at the keyboard again and read the screen. "They're late payers, but they avoid the surcharge. Just. And Doucetta's a born nickel-and-dimer, of course. It's hard to survive in small business without keeping an eye on the bottom line all the time. She's a genius at that."

A thought occurred to me. "Your employee upstairs said you had just received a shipment of juice?"

Swinford frowned. There was a tap at the door, and the same young lady who had directed us to the distillery brought in a tray with a carafe of coffee and a plate of cheese and biscuits. She handed the cups around, poured, and then took her leave. The coffee was excellent. The cheese was well aged and had a creamy texture. If the Swinford Vineyard was expanding into cheese like this, Thelma would have a significant competitor on her hands.

"Well." Jonathan leaned back in his chair. "How is the pony getting along? You've got quite a racket going there, McKenzie. I've got to hand it to you vets. Women and horses must be the bread and butter of your particular trade."

"With luck and the right farrier, the pony will be good for some years yet," I said.

"Damn," Swinford said with what he probably hoped was a man-to-man smile. "I don't begrudge my daughter the expense, mind you, but I might as well pour cash into a hole as spend it on those flippin' animals." His cell phone rang. Joe's cell phone rang. Both men took out their phones and opened them with a snap. Swinford said, "Excuse me, Dr. McKenzie. Yes? What is it, Penny. No. No. I'm off to New York tonight. Sorry.

What kind of tone are you talking about?" He cast a hurried glance at me and swiveled his chair so that his back was to us. "You're getting upset over nothing. You know I have to . . . fine. Go screw yourself." He shut the phone with a snap, swiveled his chair to face us again, and dragged up the man-to-man smile. "Women," he said. "You know, if you intend to make it big in the wine business — and I intend to make it very big — you're on the road much of the time. You have to be. My wife has a hard time with the bigger picture. But then, most women do."

"My wife does not," I said. "And I had asked about your purchase of grape juice?"

"Oh, yes, that. The thing is . . ." He leaned forward confidingly. "We can't grow enough up here to meet the demand. So yes, I buy grapes. Locally, of course. Consumers want to know that the Swinford wine is a Finger Lakes wine, but it doesn't necessarily come from acreage we actually own. A lot of the vintners do that when they run to the higher volumes." He hesitated. "But we don't publicize the fact, necessarily."

"You can count on my discretion," I said dryly.

"So. Is there anything else I can help you with?" He rose, went to the office door, and opened it.

"The night of August fourth and August sixth during the day. We're establishing the whereabouts of anyone concerned with the dairy."

He laughed, clearly at ease with this question. "I was on a buying trip in San Francisco. Got back yesterday afternoon. Well, gentlemen, if there's nothing else?"

Joe bent forward and murmured, "That was Abel Crawford on the phone. His regular vet is on vacation. He doesn't want to deal with the locum. Sounds like a prolapsed uterus."

"A barn call, is it?" Swinford said with a smile. "Good to stick with what you know, isn't it? Detective?"

Was that a sneer in the man's voice? I could think of no more questions. The prolapsed uterus at Crawford Dairy loomed. So we left and walked back up the hill to the Bronco.

"The fellow is slippery," I said, as I fastened my seat belt. "And he bears watching."

"Do you think so?" Joe said in some surprise. "He behaved like a rich jerk, sure. But that's because he is a rich jerk. What makes you think he's slippery?"

"Because we are faced with an anomaly. If we believe him, that Doucetta pays her bills on time, it makes no sense. Why pay for wine when you can't pay the vet? On the other hand, why should he lie? This goes into the 'for further consideration' column."

Joe put the key into the ignition. "Good catch. In the meantime, what's the quickest way to Crawford Dairy? It's out near the goat dairy, isn't it?"

"You can cut over to 96 by using 332," I said. "And then head south. As for Swinford, I confess to bias. The ambition, the slighting reference to his wife were somewhat distasteful, don't you think?"

Joe smiled wryly. "Doesn't make him a saboteur. Or a murderer, for that matter. He could be jerking your chain just because he can."

"True enough. The one attractive thing about the man was his affection for his daughter. That seemed real enough." I settled back in the passenger seat and set aside detection for the moment.

The Crawford Dairy was a large enterprize and was a Dairy of Distinction three years running. It was a mark of the increasing success of McKenzie Veterinary Practice, Inc. (practice limited to large animals) that we had been invited to treat one of the animals, even if it was because Abel Crawford had taken a dislike to the locum tenens.

"Snotty little kid," he said of the substitute vet when we were in the large cow barn. "Didn't listen to a word I have to say about this first calf. So I kicked his snotty little butt right out the door. Orville DeGroote had a decent word for you, Doc, so I thought I'd give you a try."

I had treated Orville DeGroote's illtempered Quarterhorse for hoof abscesses more than once and kept his cattle on an annual vaccination schedule. I was pleased that DeGroote had passed his approval on to to Crawford.

"So what it is about this heifer other than the obvious?" I asked. The cow in question was a young Holstein. She had recently calved. As is the custom in dairies like this one, the calf was taken off the mother at birth, and put into a bottle calf hut with a bucket of replacement milk and a number of other calves for company. Her uterus hung behind her hindquarters in a way that must be most uncomfortable, having emerged soon after the calf itself. There are cows prone to this problem. Joe set to work immediately, cleansing the organ with a solution of Betadine and water, sluicing it over and over again.

And what it was about the heifer was that she kicked.

"Oof!" said Joe.

"A hitch will solve that problem," I pointed out. After he straightened up and caught his breath — the heifer caught him in the midsection — I helped him fasten a rope around the cow's neck. We drew it down her flank, looped it around her right fetlock, and drew the foot up to her belly. She bellowed in a frustrated way, and then settled down.

Having been kicked a lot lower down than Joe had been in his initial efforts to put the uterus back where it belonged, the young locum had insisted on an emergency surcharge. "Not to mention he wouldn't touch the cow again without drugging her and for that he wanted another forty-five bucks," Crawford said. He shook his head. "Must think I'm made of money."

"I've yet to meet a farmer made of money."

Crawford was a big man, in the way that working farmers are big, with a solid chest, thick arms, and calloused hands. He smiled. "If you ask me, the fella was afraid of the cow."

Joe and Crawford brought a large stainless-steel tray in from the collection

236

parlor and we hoisted the uterus onto that. They held it in place just below the heifer's hindquarters, while I engaged in the lengthy process of putting the organ back where it belonged, inch by slippery inch. I placed a few stitches in the peritoneum, and the three of us stepped back. Joe released the hitch. The cow put her foot down, switched her tail, and began to eat the hay in the manger in front of her. We breathed a sigh of relief. The pesky things can slip out again with inadvertent assistance from the cow.

"Good," Crawford said briefly, when it appeared as though the uterus would stay where it belonged. "What do I owe you, Doc?"

As Joe totaled the bill, Crawford crossed his arms and put his back against the Bronco. "I hear there was some trouble up at Tre Sorelle."

"There was," I said. "Staples must have had your dairy on his inspection list. Did you run into him often?"

Crawford made a face. "Often enough. Once a month, the regs say, and he tended to poke his nose in more than that."

"Nosy, was he?" This was delicate ground. A farmer's reputation is a precious thing. If Staples had been to the dairy because of a contaminant problem, Abel would not want that bruited about.

Crawford shrugged. "Nah." His eyes narrowed. "At first I thought he might be sniffing around my Donna." Given Staples's reputation, I presumed this was either a wife or daughter, and not a cow. "But it turns out he was scouting for a cheese consortium."

"A cheese consortium?" I said.

"Yep. There's a lot of trouble west of here." He waved his arm in the general direction of Schenectady. "They're running plain out of water. Not just because of these new drought conditions from global warming, but there's just too many people using too few resources."

"By west of here, you mean California, Arizona, and Nevada," I said, just to clarify things.

"That I do. Well, we have ninety-two percent of the freshwater in the world right up here in this corner of the country, and about the best growing season for hay that you can ask for, and what better place to grow milk, nowadays? So I guess there's some big companies out there, scouting for facilities." He shrugged again. By the studied blankness of his expression, I could tell that the cheese consortium was serious business. Only the prospect of an actual profit-making activity can make a farmer poker up.

"Cow milk, only?" I said.

"Oh, no. They're after cow, sheep, goat. I'll tell you, Doc. I'm thinking seriously about converting the barns and milking goats."

This switch in topic meant the end of any further inquiry about the cheese consortium. I made a mental note to follow up with Victor. He would know whom to call. Abel pulled his cap low over his brow. "Right now, the goat cheese people are running short of milk and you wouldn't believe the demand. You think I could convert my milking enterprise?"

We had a brief discussion on the advisability of retrofitting his equipment. Yes, it could be done, but it would be a tricky matter to readjust the head guards and the vacuum press pulsator rate. There would be a third problem as the goats jumped into the pit.

Joe finished the bill and presented it to me. I turned it over to Crawford who grunted, promised to send a check, and tucked it into the top pocket of his coveralls.

Joe began packing our equipment up and I risked a final question, "Did you actually meet anyone from the cheese consortium?

Do you have an idea of what they were after?"

"What they want? They want to buy the farm, of course. They're looking for a couple of thousand acres and as many standing barns as they can find. They want to handle the whole operation, from soup to nuts, if you get my drift."

"Did you get a name before Staples was killed?"

"It wasn't Staples that was going to introduce me to the cheese people. It was Brian Folk. And I'd sure like to get my hands on the yahoo that sent him to glory. I was looking at making a decent price off this place for the first time in my life."

"Indeed? You would sell out a business that's been in your family for, how long is it?"

"A hundred and fifty years, give or take a decade." He pushed his John Deere hat back and rubbed his forehead. "The days of the family farm are over, Doc. I can't push enough volume through here to make more than enough to pay my taxes and keep the family in groceries. I'm tired. I'm whipped. And I'm getting too damn old to work as hard as I have to get that dollar. You ask anyone farming in New York state, and they'll tell you the same thing. The only way out is to have some big agri-company waltz in and add you to their stable. That cheese company makes me the right kind of offer, I'm out of here in a flash.

"Tell you another thing, Doc. That Folk was real interested in getting those people in to see Doucetta Capretti."

ELEVEN

"So it is the evil real estate people after all!" Ally said with some excitement. "Hold still, Maddy. I can't get this clip fastened in your hair."

"Cheese," I said, "not real estate. And it is merely a lead." I sat in my chair on the porch and sipped some of Victor's Scotch. Madeline and I were almost ready for our dinner at the Summersville Country Club with the Berglands. Madeline was splendid in a flowery caftan. Her auburn hair was swept off the back of her neck and onto her head in an attractive topknot. It is thick and heavy, and the clip that Allegra succeeded in snapping closed kept slipping free.

"There," Ally said. "You look beautiful."

"I just want to feel cool," Madeline said, fanning herself with a copy of *Cows Today*. "It's so hot and still it must be coming on to storm." We all looked over the porch railing to the horizon. Black clouds massed in the west. Madeline sat down, still fanning herself. "I made some pretty good progress myself on the case, guys. First off, Thelma found a good spot for her store."

"On Main?" I asked.

"Oh, not here in Summersville. We drove into Hemlock Falls. You know what a tourist destination that's getting to be. She found a nice spot right next to the hardware store. A beautiful old cobblestone building. We're lookin' at it tomorrow. But *that's* not especially helpful to the case. You're going to like this, sweetie. The guy that's showin' it to us is the head of the accounting firm that handles the dairy business. And," she added triumphantly, "you and I and Victor and Thelma have an appointment to see the store tomorrow afternoon!"

"Excellent work," I said. "You must have been reading my mind, my dear. I had that very thought this afternoon, or something like it."

"Now, I'll tell you what's even more interesting. Thelma went out and bought a bunch of office equipment. She's already kicked Victor out of his den and set up shop. I have to say, sweetie, I haven't seen her this good-tempered in all the time we've known her. Anyhow, she said we were goin' to 'take the initial meeting with Mr. Raintree' over the phone. So we had a conference call, which just was me on one line and Thelma on the other but she wanted to be taken seriously, and I don't blame her. Anyhow, when Thelma told John Raintree that she was interested in maybe makin' her own cheese for the store he chuckled some."

"Chuckled some?"

"He didn't come right out and say it, but he figured we'd be better off buying shares in the Brooklyn Bridge. He did ask if she was a person who liked to take risks."

"Indeed." This fit in with Crawford's impassioned diatribe about how hard it was to make a living in farming. As for Swinford, we had an old expression that covered his behavior during the interview: he was trying one on. In any event, I was beginning to wonder if Doucetta had another source of income to support the lifestyle of her family members. "What about the retail store?"

"I made Thelma describe the store she wanted to exactly fit the retail operation at Tre Sorelle. He wasn't quite so gloomy about that. He quieted up some when I made a comment about all the cash that lies around places like that and how maybe the government wouldn't care if some of it fell off the table and into our pockets. With a little nudging he let us see that it could be a pretty good sum. Maybe enough to buy half of a Mercedes. But he's an honest man, that's for sure."

"Very useful information, my dear. Very useful. And the appointment with him tomorrow is a stroke of genius."

Ally tucked a curl behind Madeline's ear. She smiled at both of us and said, "Thank you, Ally. How did you get on with Ashley today?"

An odd look passed over Allegra's pretty face. Madeline stopped fanning abruptly. "What is it, sweetie?"

"I got the job done. I'll make out a schedule of who was where in the dairy the day of each murder. Ashley's got a retentive memory, which helps a lot. Do you want me to go over it now?"

"Why don't we wait for Joe?" Madeline suggested. "We'll have a staff meeting after we get back from the country club. It shouldn't be much past nine o'clock. Is there something else bothering you?"

"It's just a feeling, really. Nothing Ashley actually said. But her father keeps pretty close tabs on her, or rather," Ally corrected herself, "Ashley thinks he does. He got on her case about the milk inspector." She frowned. "Ashley swears she didn't do more than go out and have a beer with him. . . ."

"With Melvin Staples?" I said. "The man's a swine."

"Ashley's only eighteen," Madeline said rather worriedly.

"I know, I know." Ally's dimples showed in a quick smile. "The drinking age in New York is twenty-one. But in other states, it's eighteen. Anyhow. Her dad pitched a fit. Insisted on dropping her off and picking her up from work when he was in town to make sure Mel wasn't hanging around. And he made her mother do it when he was off on a trip. Ashley was pretty fried about it all."

I made a note in my case file. "Very interesting. Certainly a more comprehensible motive for Staples's murder than the nefarious cheese consortium. I am not a fan of conspiracy theories and find it hard to believe an entire business organization is dedicated to murder."

"Oh, I don't know," Ally said. "What about Murder, Incorporated? What about the Mafia? What about . . ."

I held up my hand. "We will pursue it further when we return tonight. The Hackney Sunny gets just twenty cc's of bute tonight, by the way. I left a note on the treatment sheet on the stall door. And let's schedule the farrier for a trim."

Allegra headed off to the clinic rounds and Madeline and I headed out to dinner. And the storm she'd predicted rolled right in.

The wind came up. The rain began slowly, in pudgy drops that splattered against the windshield like overfed bugs. Thunder rolled, and lightning cracked the sky with violence. By the time we reached the club grounds, it was raining hard and the air had cooled considerably.

The Summersville Country Club has an attractive facility on a hundred acres just east of the village. The clubhouse sits over a man-made lake — created from swamp grounds when the building was erected — and is surrounded on three sides by golf greens. Golfers in electric carts were fleeing the rain as we came up the circular drive. I dropped Madeline off at the entrance and parked some way from the building. By the time I returned to escort her inside, my umbrella was drenched through.

Madeline smoothed the collar of my seersucker sports coat, and we went inside to find Victor and Thelma. They sat at a table in front of the long picture window that faced the lake. I had asked Victor to make sure the Celestines joined us for dinner, and so they had. The look Victor gave me as I seated Madeline was fulminating.

"You're late," he snarled.

"We are not," I responded.

"Hello, Dr. McKenzie!" Caterina said. She smiled hesitantly at Madeline. "I'm so glad you can join us. It's not often we have guests here at the club."

Looking pleased with himself, Frank let out a long burp. "Bet you're surprised to see me here, Doc."

"Not at all," I said. "I assume that Simon released you on your own recognizance?"

"He released me 'cause I've got a good Jew lawyer."

"That's it," Victor said. "We're leaving." He pushed himself away from the table.

I held up my hand. "A moment, Victor. If you'd accompany me to the bar so that I may get Madeline a drink, I'd appreciate it."

Victor's lips were tight, but he said, "I'd be delighted. Madeline? What may I get for you?"

"Just a glass of wine, thank you." She was looking at Celestine with a kind of horrified fascination.

"And we'll have another round," Frank said. "Just ask old Jim for Frank's usual."

Victor jerked me toward the bar. There were several patrons ahead of us, so we joined the queue. "Who *is* that guy?" Victor hissed furiously. "Thelma's about ready to slug him, and for once I don't blame her. I'd like to slug him myself."

"I told you this afternoon when I requested your assistance. He figures in my current case."

"Your curr— you mean that damn fool detective agency?" Victor snorted. "I thought you were talking about some clinical problem you're having with a patient." He breathed heavily through his nose. "You're going to owe me big-time after this, McKenzie." His face was red with suppressed annoyance.

"You already owe me big-time," I retorted. "And if you don't calm down, you're going to give yourself a stroke."

"I'll worry about my own arteries, thank you very much. And how do you figure I owe you the price of a piece of bubble gum, much less a couple of hours with the biggest turkey it's ever been my misfortune to meet? The man's totally put me off my feed."

"You could stand to lose a few pounds," I said somewhat unfeelingly. "As to your obligation — I have three words for you: Thelma. Inheritance. Cheese."

Some of the high color left Victor's face.

"You mean Madeline putting Thelma on to that retail business."

"I do."

He looked thoughtful. We placed our order at the bar. As we wended our way back to the tables, drinks in hand, he muttered, "Fine. But we're even now, right?"

"You were gone so long I thought you died and fell in!" Frank chortled.

We settled down to endure the meal. Between the shrimp starter and the salad, Frank boasted of cheating those customers befuddled enough to hire Celestine Builders for their building projects. Between the salad and the entrée, he told us Doucetta had an offer to buy the dairy from some big company out west, but that Doucetta had turned them down flat. In the course of noisily consuming the dessert, we learned that Doucetta refused to make a will, which was the only thing that kept him, Frank, from whacking the old lady upside the head. Madeline made valiant attempts to change the subject. Caterina was touchingly eloquent about the return of her sons, for example, but Frank kept dragging the conversation to his mother-in-law. The poor woman appeared to be his bête noire.

"The old bat's just a superstitious peasant," he said. " 'Fraid if she makes her will, it'll catch death's eye or some kind of crap like that. So who gets the Capretti millions? The wife, here, and her stuck-up sister. I know the law. I checked it all out. The old lady goes toes up intestate, that's what they call it, intestate, the money's split between Cater-eeen-ah and that bat-brained Anna Luisa. The way I figure it, I stick around long enough, some of it's bound to fall into my wallet." He giggled and slurped the rest of his vodka.

"Frank," Caterina said desperately, "maybe you'd like some coffee?"

"Shut up," he said. He didn't look at her, but leered at *my* wife, who was looking especially beautiful in the candlelight. "I'd like some of what Madeline's having."

Thelma and Victor stood it all the way through dessert. But as soon as the coffee had been served, they rose as one, flinging excuses at us with an air of throwing themselves from a sinking ship. Needless to say, Madeline remained gracious and smiling throughout.

"Okay, so it was worth it," Madeline admitted as we made our way home. "Did you see the look Caterina gave him when he let it slip about the big offer for the dairy? But I swear I don't know why Caterina puts up with him. I mean, she's nice enough, but honestly, Austin, the man is just about intolerable."

The torrent of rain had lessened to a drizzle. Somewhere in the distance, the fire alarms sounded; a consequence, I was sure, of the violent display of lightning from the storm. The roads were slick with rain, and I slowed to accommodate the poor conditions.

"I suppose Caterina's faith has something to do with it," I observed. "But having dinner with them was a horrible experience. I apologize for putting you through it."

"The worst." Madeline glanced at me and put her hand over mine. "What are you looking so pleased about, sweetie?"

I covered her hand with my own. "The very beautiful Marietta seems to be in the clear."

"My goodness," Madeline said, "you suspected her?"

"No one is excluded until the truth is uncovered," I said, rather grandly. "The odious Frank is right; New York state law mandates the estate of the deceased to the next of kin. Spouse, sons and daughters, brothers, sisters. The law of inheritance goes straight down, stopping at the first line of family, so to speak. With a living aunt and mother, Marietta wouldn't get a thing. If her motive was to shut the dairy down to force a sale and reap the benefit of the profits, we now know that it is a motive no longer."

"So the list of suspects is narrowing," Madeline said. "Thank goodness for that."

We arrived home at about nine thirty, to find Joe and Allegra at the kitchen table, surrounded by sheets of paper and consumed with gloom.

"It looks like nobody did it," Allegra said with exasperation as we walked in. "Look. Here's the Staples's murder. I made a time line down the x-axis of the chart, and the y-axis is the people at the dairy. The barn help went straight from the milking parlor to the cheesery. They have a bunch of stuff to do there every day and the routine doesn't seem to vary much.

"You were right about Pietro and Tony." She blushed a little. It was clear the boys had found it a delight to aid Allegra in her part of the investigation. "They helped me talk to them, and it's pretty clear none of them were anywhere near the milk room between nine and nine thirty. The alibis for the Folk murder aren't as tight, of course, because we aren't sure what time he was killed the night before he was discovered, but they all sleep in the same three-bedroom house on the farm, and they swear they were together eating dinner, watching TV, like that." She scowled at the papers. "So that leaves Mrs. Capretti, Marietta, Caterina and Frank, and Ashley herself. Mrs. Capretti was yelling at the rest of her family the morning of the Staples murder, and Ashley says she saw them all pouring out of the house once she ran outside and started screaming. She's very sure about that."

"And the night before the discovery of Folk's body?" I asked.

"Caterina went to pick Pietro and Tony up at the airport. They got back around two. The flight was late. I checked, by the way, and it was. Marietta and Mrs. Capretti watched TV, they said, and they were there when the bartender from the club brought Mr. Celestine home."

I sat next to Ally and perused the sheets myself. "According to the forensics report, the clumps of soil under Folk's fingernails place him at the high school parking lot," I said. "That's twelve miles from the dairy. The murderer had to kill him there, and then transport him all the way to the compost pile in back of the goat barn. Whoever did it had to have at least an hour to make that trip." I resisted the impulse to crumple to sheets into a ball and put them into the garbage disposal. Lincoln, sensing my frustration, pawed at me and barked.

"We'll take a walk in a few moments, old fellow."

"So, like I said, nobody did it." Ally threw her hands up in the air in a theatrical gesture. "There weren't any bodies, nope. It's all an illusion."

I leaned back in my chair. "There are two possibilities here. The first is that the two murders are totally unconnected. This is possible, but in my view, not probable. My initial theory was that the two men got in the way of the saboteur, and the saboteur eliminated them. If the sabotage and the murders are not related, the same theory holds. Folk knew who killed Staples and blackmailed him. Or her," I added, to forestall protests from my wife and our young protégé. "In short, I believe there is only one murderer.

"Now we do have three possible suspects in the Staples murder who are unconnected to the dairy. Jonathan Swinford has a possible motive if he discovered a relationship between his just-barely-of-age daughter and Staples."

"Ashley and Staples?" Joe said. "That's disgusting. He was what — thirty-five, thirty-six?"

I went on. " "Which brings us to the other motive. Jealousy."

"Ashley said her father beat Melvin Staples up," Ally said. "Now, she didn't see it happen, but Mel said something to her about her father's temper. And then the autopsy report showed those old bruises on his face."

"Parental rage. Not precisely jealous, but close enough. We would consider Mrs. Staples, if she hadn't been in Syracuse with her mother-in-law. And of course, there are the Brandstetters. The testimony of Anna Luisa's downstairs neighbor is clear. Luisa was in that rented apartment twenty miles away all morning. The one without a verifiable alibi is Neville."

Nobody looked at me. Then Ally said, in rather a small voice, "But he's the client."

"He is indeed." I cleared my throat. Brandstetter was a friend and colleague. "This line of inquiry must be followed up. It's essential that we discover more about Folk before we jump to any conclusions. Presumably, he has a wife, whom we shall interview, and the use of a part-time secretary courtesy of the village. I'll start with the village."

"I thought Lieutenant Provost was handling that end of the investigation," Allegra said.

"He may have overlooked something." I had an uncomfortable thought. What if Simon was right? What if the murders were connected to whatever nefarious hijinks the two had been up to?

"And what about the sabotage?" Joe asked.

Now, that was worse yet. I had a theory about the sabotage. "We had dinner tonight with the Celestines," I began.

Ally looked at Joe. Solemnly, they both began to applaud. "We figured you deserve it after sitting through dinner with that jerk," Joe said with a grin.

"Thank you. What I deserve, in fact, is another inch of Victor's excellent Scotch." I excused myself from the table, went to the small cabinet that serves us as a wine cupboard, and poured myself a healthy measure. I came back to the table and resumed my postulations.

"I was struck with Pietro and Tony's loyalty to their mother when I first met them yesterday," I said. "They are quick to defend her from their skunk of a father. Tonight we heard how loving a mother Caterina is to her sons. I believe, in short, that Caterina is the saboteur. She wants her sons back. She wants her mother to accept them into the business. And she played on the superstitions of the old lady with the contamination of the high somatic cell count." I paused and took a breath. It is at such times that I wished I smoked a pipe. "It was a curse, she told her mother, and the curse would be lifted when her boys came home and they did and it was."

"So Caterina's the saboteur?" Madeline said. "Austin, you are a genius!"

"Thank you, my dear."

"No offense, Doc," Ally said. "But we don't really have proof."

"I have little doubt that the poor woman will confess, if pressed," I said. "Madeline seems to be in her confidence; it would be a good thing if you verified it, if possible, my dear. Ally is quite right. There is no proof. And perhaps now that her boys are home, Caterina won't need to plague the dairy anymore. If the sabotage stops, we can infer a great deal from that."

The phone rang. I frowned in its direction. A call this late at night meant an animal emergency. "I'll get it," Joe said. He rose and took the receiver into the living room.

"I hope it's not the Swinfords with another foundered horse," Ally said wryly. "Ashley and her mother just can't seem to stop thinking of the horses as big house pets with the digestion systems of pigs."

Our idle conversation came to a halt when Joe came back into the room. The expression on his face was serious. "That was Rita."

"My column," I said. "Good heavens. I completely forgot to send it in. The topic this week is sarcoptic mange, and I've been unable to find a suitable photograph to accompany it."

"She didn't mention the article. She said there's been a fire at the Tre Sorelle Dairy. Half of the buildings are gone."

We were shocked into silence.

Madeline's first impulse was to rush to the scene of the fire to see if we could help. "I don't care how tough Mrs. Capretti is, Austin. She's ninety-four years old!" She rubbed her forehead tiredly, "No, no. We'd probably just be in the way. But I know what we can do. I can call Trudy Schlegleman at the Ladies Auxiliary and tell her we can put up anyone who needs putting up."

"Including the goats?" Ally said. "Thank God they were all out at pasture." Ally looked at me in alarm. "They were, weren't they?"

"It's more than likely." And if the animals had gone up in flames with the buildings, we would know about it soon enough. There was no need to torment the child with bad dreams.

"Did Rita say anyone was hurt?" Madeline asked Joe.

"She said there weren't any casualties." He glanced Ally's way. "I'm assuming she meant animals as well as people, but she wasn't specific. I can call her back."

"I'll call Trudy," Madeline said firmly. "Her husband's chief of the volunteers and she'll know what's what." She took the phone away.

"Rita said it was arson?" I asked Joe.

"Rita said there was a fire. She didn't say anything more." He looked as grim as I felt. "We might have been wrong about that curse."

Suddenly, I felt very tired. I took my dog and went out to say good night to my horse.

Twelve

"No people were hurt, thank goodness," Rita said when I put in a call to her in the morning. "But some of the goats died of smoke inhalation. At least I hope it was smoke inhalation. They always tell you that and I never believe a word of it."

"You're being unnecessarily glum," I said. "Statistically . . ."

"Don't give me statistically. You didn't see those poor little bodies. I went out with Nigel to cover the fire. Sometimes I hate this business. I don't suppose you'd want to do a serious column on how to protect your animals from fire."

"Of course," I said. "But I didn't call you to discuss the column."

"And speaking of the column, Austin, the sarcoptic mange thing was perfectly revolting. I did as you asked. I Googled for photos and I'm telling you right here and now I am *not* running a photo of that stuff in a family-oriented newspaper."

"Rita, you are displacing."

"What?"

"It's engaging in an activity or behavior to avoid another activity or behavior. Horses weave to avoid anxiety, or that's the theory, anyway."

"I know what displacement is, Austin," she said sharply. Then, more mildly, she added, "And you're right. I don't want to talk about the fire. You know they took poor old Doucetta to the hospital."

"I thought you said there were no human casualties."

"She pitched a fit over the damage, I guess, and couldn't catch her breath. So they took her in for observation. I called over there just now. They said she's resting comfortably, whatever *that* means. I believe that as much as I believe everybody in a fire dies of smoke inhalation and not third-degree burns." Rita ran out of breath, so she stopped talking.

"Has the cause of the fire been established?"

"I was hoping you could tell me. I couldn't get a word out of Trudy Schlegleman's husband. And I can't reach Simon."

"He's probably not answering his cell phone."

"He'll answer his cell phone if you call him," Rita said. "Do you realize what an impediment to investigative journalism cell phones are? The person I'm trying to reach can always tell it's me so they don't even answer." She sighed. "I suppose I'd better go out there again. If I come and pick you up, will you come with me?"

I cast a glance at the clinic appointments on the refrigerator. There was a routine animal health check scheduled for the Longacre's Longhorn cattle. Joe and Allegra could handle that with ease. Most important was the meeting in Hemlock Falls with the dairy's accountant. "Yes, I'll come with you. But I'll meet you there. Madeline and I have an appointment later in the afternoon."

"She's already out there with the volunteers, isn't she? She can drive you back." She hung up before I could protest.

Rita was at the door in twenty minutes. Madeline was with the Ladies Auxiliary, planning support for the victims of the fire, both animals and human. Joe and Ally were in the barn attending to the animals. I left a note on the refrigerator door, with instructions on the interstate health certificate, and we left for the site of the fire.

Fire. If there is one word that can panic the most phlegmatic of farmers, that's it.

Practicing veterinarians are no strangers to barn fires. Old barns have old wiring. Vermin gnaw through new wiring. When anxious farmers store new hay in tightly packed bales too soon after cutting, it can be highly combustible, and more than one hay barn has spontaneously ignited and burned to the ground. And it is always quite dreadful to see the results.

The thunderstorm had left hot, muggy weather in its wake, and the air seemed to hug the ground. The smell hung in the air at least two miles out. The odor of a barn fire is distinctive. It is mainly damp wood, ash, melted plastic, and often, tragically, roasted flesh.

Rita let out a sigh of relief as we came up the slight rise that led to the dairy. "It looks like it was the creamery, mostly, and the milking barns. Thank God it didn't get to the goat barns. And the house looks okay. Bit singed around the lawn."

In addition to the fifteen or so automobiles parked every which way on the lawn, a Summersville Fire Department truck sat parked in front of the ruined creamery. Two figures in the long rubber coats, high rubber boots, and protective helmets of the fireman's uniform tramped heavily through the ashes. A number of volunteers were at work in the goat barns. The bleats and cheery shouts coming from that direction suggested that the does were being milked by hand.

"Looking for smoldering piles, do you suppose?" Rita said, nodding at the two suited figures. "Think they'd know anything about the source of the fire?" She braked, turned the ignition off, and sat for a moment, taking things out of her tote bag and putting other things in. I got out of the passenger side and approached the nearest rubber figure. He took his helmet off.

"Rassmussen," I said.

"Doc," he nodded. " 'Fraid there's not too much to do here, but it's good of you to come and help. Doc Tallant's already been and gone. Wasn't too bad, considering. Lost three goat kids, a buck, and a couple of does."

"No people," Rita said, coming up behind me. "You can confirm that?"

Gordy turned and pointed. "They're all over there. Except for Mrs. Capretti and the herd manager and his people."

We were perhaps a hundred yards from the dairy office. Marietta, Caterina, Pietro, Tony, and Frank stood in an awkward clot at the fire-darkened office door. Marietta raised a hand in salute. I waved back. Then she and the two boys disappeared into the office. Buckled by the heat, the door failed to close behind them.

"They took Doucetta to the ER last night to check her out," Gordy said, "but she made such a fuss they brought her back. But that granddaughter of hers made her stay in bed. So she's up to the house. The barn help's in the barn."

Rita took her tape recorder from her tote and held it up. "Have you determined a cause of the fire yet, Mr. Rassmussen?"

"This for attribution?" he asked with a wry smile. He had clearly been there all night. His face ran with sweat. Ash smeared his forehead. He smelled of fatigue.

"Of course it's for attribution," Rita said.

"Then let me get out of this rig first, will you? Cripes, it's hot!" He shrugged himself out of the overcoat and overalls and kicked his boots off. He padded over to the fire truck in his stocking feet, retrieved his shoes and a bottle of water from a compartment near the neatly coiled hose, and sat down on the ground. "Whew!"

"Bad one?" Rita asked sympathetically,

"Could have been worse," Gordy said. "But I'm beat. You can put in that article of yours that the volunteer firefighters of Summersville did one hell of a job, though."

Rita smiled. "I've already got a list of names. Nigel's out right now getting pictures. You can bet we'll give them a pat on the back. We have a pretty good shot of the fire at its height. I'm going to run it front page, above the fold, with a whacking big headline: 'Summersville Volunteers in a Blaze of Glory.' " She struggled with a small surge of emotion. "I think you guys are as brave as all get out."

"Huh," Gordy said. He took a long swallow of water and coughed.

"As do I," I offered.

Both of them ignored me.

"So you guys must have some idea of how this happened."

Gordy wiped his nose with his forearm and stared at Frank Celestine. Celestine stood with his legs planted wide, and his arms folded across his chest. Caterina sat on the front stoop, her hands in her lap. She looked like a sleepwalker. "That one" — he jerked his thumb in Frank's direction — "says it's lightning. Lightning," he added in disgust.

"There was quite a storm last night," I said.

"Yeah. But was it raining gasoline?"

"So it was arson," Rita said. "Any idea who set the fire?"

"We're pulling out all the stops on this one. Provost called in the state arson squad." Gordy looked up at the sky, as if expecting a helicopter to descend momentarily. "And they're supposed to be here any time now. Part of how come Riley and me are still here is to keep the site blocked off from anyone who's nosing around." He gestured toward the center of the T, where most of the destruction appeared to have occurred. The area was cordoned off by the familiar yellow police tape. Riley, if it were he in the concealing overcoat, tramped around the perimeter in a guardlike fashion.

Rita shoved the tape recorder closer to Gordy's mouth. "Can you tell me a little bit about the type of evidence that made you realize the fire was set?"

"I guess," Gordy said, a little uneasily. "It's not supposed to be secret, is it?"

Rita grinned at him. "With some twenty volunteer firemen running around here last night, you don't expect to keep it a secret long, do you?"

"You got a point there, Santelli."

"Thank you, Rassmussen."

They stood and smiled at each other. I had an odd feeling of being superfluous. Madeline tells me I am somewhat insensitive to the more subtle signs human beings use to communicate with one another. Since embarking upon the career of investigating detective, I've made considerable effort to improve in this area. Rita was a widow. Gordy was a divorcé. I made a deduction. "Are you dating one another?" I asked, to ease the silence.

Rita's freckles disappeared in a tide of red. Gordy took a large gulp of water and had a coughing fit. Rita turned off the tape recorder with a decisive jab of her thumb and glared at me. "Any other social clunkers you want to drop into the conversation, McKenzie?"

"Ah, no," I said.

"Bottles with rags stuffed in the neck," Gordy said loudly. "We found gasoline-soaked rags, and a lot of shattered bottle glass. Hard to say how many. But more than six or seven, that's for sure."

"Really?" I said. This was very interesting. "A Molotov cocktail sort of affair?"

"I guess so." Gordy looked doubtful. "You don't think Russians set the fire, do you?"

"What Russians would that be?" I asked rather tartly.

Gordy was saved from the embarrassment of a reply by the arrival of two black Ford LTDs and Simon's Ford Escort. The investigators from Syracuse had arrived.

Rita headed straight to the arson team. Gordy trailed after her. Frank's head came up, and he jogged after them, avid curiosity in his face. I deliberated a moment. Under some gentle persuasion, Provost would fill me in on the fire forensics. And if I had to endure any more of Celestine's company, it would have to be under less trying circumstances. Now might be a good time to discover if anyone from the dairy had a clue as to how the fire was set.

Caterina stood as I came up to the office door and gave me a small smile. "It's probably the wrong time to say so, but I really enjoyed meeting Madeline last night."

"Madeline is a delight," I agreed. "I take it you're all right?"

"Me?" She looked down at herself, as if astonished I'd asked. She wore a droopy sort of skirt and white blouse. A Tre Sorelle scarf was wrapped around her head. She touched it. "Tony said I should wear this to keep the ashes out of my hair." The smile she gave me this time was much more confident. "He's such a good son to me."

"I'm sorry for all your trouble." I turned to look at the devastation.

"Tony says it's not as bad as it looks, although he said not to say so to anyone else." She added in a whisper. "The insurance, you know. Tony says they'll try to wriggle out of paying us if they can."

"Hm," I said. "Tell me, when did the fire start?"

She widened her eyes. "We didn't know a thing was happening 'til we got back here after dinner last night."

"What time would that have been?"

"About two, I think. Frank likes to stay until closing. He thinks it shows support for the club."

I let this one pass.

"By the time we got here, the fire was almost out. Everyone was milling around in this confused way." She trailed off. "I didn't know what to do, exactly, so I got Frank to bed. . . ."

I let this one pass, too. The man was undoubtedly dead drunk.

"And then I made coffee for everybody. Sandwiches, too. The volunteers were about starved to death. And then Mamma had this sort of attack." Her hand went to her chest. "The firefighters made her get into the ambulance. Of course, she didn't want to go." Then she added earnestly, "She really feels the loss of her cane, you know. Is there any way you can talk Lieutenant Provost into getting it back fast? She's using this aluminum thing now, and she says it's too light to be any use at all."

"I'll see what I can do," I promised. "Who was home when the fire started?"

"Home? Um. Marietta had a date. The volunteers called her on her cell phone and she came right back. The guy came right along with her."

I drew my notepad from my pocket. "Do you remember his name?"

"Um. Let's see. It's that nice doctor from the clinic at Hemlock Falls. Andy Bishop, that's his name. He was the one that took a look at Mamma when she started that scary coughing and said she should go to the ER. Anyway, he left, and Marietta started making phone calls. The whole milking system's been just trashed, and we've got all these does to dry off. She thought maybe she could get some help with the injections. We have over five hundred milking does, you know."

"You mean the volunteers in the sheds aren't milking the does?" I said. "They're drying them off?" Two injections of lincomycin spectinomycin two days apart accomplish this quite successfully.

Caterina jumped. My tone must have been stern. "Well, yes, the poor things. They can't walk around all bagged up. Their udders could burst."

"I'm well aware of that, Caterina." I took a breath to calm down. "But you do realize what a disaster this is for the dairy. The only way to get the does up and milking again is to rebreed them. Gestation is five months. Tre Sorelle won't be producing for five months until the kids are weaned."

Caterina's mouth formed a soft *O*.

I pushed open the door to the dairy office. Caterina followed me. Marietta sat huddled behind the desk. Her face was haggard. "My dear girl," I said. "I am so sorry. But was this really necessary?"

She nodded mutely. Then she said, "What else could we do?"

"Borrow the milking machines, of course."

"From where?" Caterina interrupted bitterly. "We had ten. You tell me who'll lend us ten goat-milking machines soon enough to save five hundred does."

Pietro and Tony stood at the window, looking out at the activity in the sheds. I still wasn't sure which one was which. The taller one turned and came up to me, hand extended. "Thank you for coming, Dr. McKenzie."

"You're quite welcome," I said, shaking his hand. "I just wish there were more that I could do. Are you *quite* sure you want to dry the goats off?"

"Pete and I couldn't see any other way out of this particular mess."

So the taller one was Tony. He had a more aquiline nose than his brother did. Neither resembled their father in the least. A fortunate circumstance, in my opinion.

"Please sit down, Dr. McKenzie." Pietro drew a chair from the corner and set it close to the desk. "My mother, as usual, is quick with the food." He gestured at the coffee urn and a pile of cookies on a plate next to it. "May I get you a cup of coffee?"

"Thank you. Black, if you would."

He poured it into a foam cup and handed it to me. "She was out in the shed setting up coffee and cake for the volunteers before the sun was up," he said rather ruefully.

"Your mother," I said.

"Yes. And Mrs. McKenzie, too? She's the curvy lady with the reddish hair?"

"Er, yes."

He flung his hands wide in a very European gesture. "She'd have a hard time getting down the street whistle-free back home," he said. "My uncles like a lady of substance."

"No offense," Tony added. "And with all due respect."

"Shall we leave it at that?" I asked dryly. "And 'back home' is Italy, and not here?"

They exchanged glances. "We decided to emigrate just after college," Pietro said. "We grew up speaking Italian here, of course, *Donna* Doucetta insisted. And when we ran into a little trouble here . . ."

"Kid stuff." His brother shrugged.

"*Donna* Doucetta made it pretty clear we needed kind of a cooling-off period. So she sent us to live with her brothers in Siena."

Tony smiled. "Italy treated us pretty good. And we never looked back."

"Until now," Pietro said. He looked out the window at the courtyard. His father had returned from the goat sheds. He stood in front of Caterina. His mouth was going, and we couldn't hear what he said, but Caterina shook her head and backed away.

"I warned him," Pietro said in a tight voice.

"Go," Tony said.

Pietro made the office door in two strides and flung himself into the yard. His father retreated as soon as Pietro came down the steps and shambled off toward the house.

Tony looked at me and shrugged. "He just needs a little reminding now and then. It's all about respect."

"We heard the sirens last night," I said, rather abruptly. "About ten thirty."

"Yeah. We were watching a DVD up at the

house, just kind of enjoying the storm, you know?"

"You and Pete."

"Right. And then Aunt Luisa came running in screaming that the goats started raising a ruckus. You know how they get."

Goats were an excellent early-warning system. But I wasn't concerned with the goats at the moment. "Your Aunt Luisa? You mean Anna Luisa Brandstetter?"

He made a wry face. "The screamer. Yeah. She showed up here yesterday about dinnertime with a pile of suitcases and not enough tissue."

My face must have shown my bewilderment.

"Crying, sobbing, shrieking, you name it. She had a fight with Neville. Told *Donna* Doucetta she was moving back home. Pete and I hauled her suitcases into a bedroom and she shut herself up for a while. We could still hear her though. And then Neville shows up."

"Neville Brandstetter?"

"You think there's more than one guy named Neville in Summersville?" he said impatiently. "Yeah. Neville shows up. They go back into her bedroom. They scream. They shout. *Donna* Doucetta marches in and starts yelling at the both of them. He leaves. That's it."

I was silent. This was a very distressing development.

"So," Tony said, getting back to his story. "Aunt Luisa comes out saying the goats are yelling. I walked out onto the balcony and saw this flickering, like, right where the milking parlor was. I yelled at Pete to call nine-one-one and ran down the hill like the devil himself was after me. By the time I got here, the whole center part of the dairy was whoosh!" He flicked his fingers in the air. "You ever been close to a fire, Dr. McKenzie? The heat it gives off is amazing. The herdsman and the barn help take the van into the village on Wednesday nights after the seven thirty milking 'cause that's when the movie changes at the theater. There wasn't a heck of a lot just the two of us could do and of course, Aunt Luisa's just useless. We had a couple of meningeal does in the back with their kids and we tried to pull them out but it was nothing doing." He paused. "You've got one heck of a fire department here, I'll give you that. Those guys were here in about fifteen minutes. It was amazing. I didn't think a small town like this one could get a turnout like that. I'll bet there were twenty guys here. A couple of women, too."

The phone rang, startling all three of us. Marietta had been sitting silent throughout Tony's summary. She picked the phone up, listened for a moment, and then said, "Thank you," in such a heartfelt tone, that I knew she had been strung very tightly. She hung up and looked at her cousin. "That was Jonathan. He said they've finished with the does. Isn't that amazing? So fast. It's all happened so fast." She fell silent.

"That's my man," Tony said.

"Jonathan?" I said. "Jonathan Swinford?"

"Yes. He showed up this morning with the volunteers to help with the goats." She smiled at me. "Along with Madeline, of course. You should have seen your wife, Dr. McKenzie. She had everyone organized into teams and had the goats moving through the chutes in nothing flat. And she ordered me out of the barn. Said I'd be of more help later on. With Grandmamma." She looked around, as if a bell had rung. "I'd better go up and check on her. She's supposed to stay in bed, but it's like trying to keep a helium balloon from rising to the ceiling."

"May I go with you?"

"You know, I think she'll be glad to see you."

I turned to Tony as I went out the door. "What time did Dr. Brandstetter leave the house?"

He thought a minute. "Maybe a half hour before Aunt Luisa told us about the goats. He was some pissed off, I can tell you."

I followed Marietta up the hill in a somber mood.

"So it's you, arsehole," Doucetta said. She sat up in a king-sized bed, frail and unbearably sad. Anna Luisa, looking like an unmown lawn after a heavy rain, sat in a chair near the bed. It was a spectacular room, filled with heavily ornate furniture and with a view of the valley. Doucetta waved her aluminum cane. "They are trying to kill my dairy."

Luisa got up and rustled toward her mother. She wore a diaphanous sort of negligee and her hair was uncombed. "Now, Mamma, just settle down. The fire's out. We only lost three goats and five kids. The rest of the does are just fine."

Doucetta glared at me. "This daughter is as stupid as the other one." She waved her hand at Luisa dismissively. It was as gnarled as the roots of a banyan tree. "The goats that burned up were meningeal goats. They were dead anyway."

"Mamma! I can't believe you're this coldhearted!" Luisa flounced to her chair.

Marietta smiled to herself and began to straighten the clutter on the nightstand. I smoothed my mustache. Meningeal goats are infected with deer worm, which is usually a fatal condition. Even in crisis, Doucetta could not be accused of sentimentality.

"Coldhearted? I have to be coldhearted. They are trying to kill my dairy." Two tears rolled down her cheeks. Her bright black eyes were cloudy. She closed them, and lay so still that for a moment, I feared she had fainted.

"Do you have any idea who could have set the fire, Mrs. Capretti?"

Her eyes snapped open. "That tax inspector."

"He's dead, Grandmamma," Marietta said.

"I know he's dead, you idiot. He kept nosing around here like a stray cat after garbage. He wanted me to sell out to the cheese people. I said hell, no. You want to know who set fire to my dairy? The cheese people did." She glared at me. She sat straight up among the pillows. "You!" she said. "You're a detective. *Es vero?*"

"If you are asking me if that's true," I said cautiously, "yes, Mrs. Capretti, I am."

"Go after the cheese people and smack them around! I want you to find out who is trying to kill my dairy!" Her bony fingers worked the fringe on the bedspread. "Who is trying to kill me!"

I looked at Marietta, alarmed. "Someone has threatened her life?"

"No, no. She means that the dairy *is* her life." Marietta looked down at her grandmother with an expression equal parts affection and exasperation. Doucetta raised her aluminum cane, looked at it in disgust, and flung it across the room. "I want my cane back, too!" she shouted. "There is a curse on this house until my cane is returned!"

"I thought the curse was lifted when the boys came by," Marietta said. "So there's another curse?"

Doucetta pointed at her. "You! You can go too far!"

"That's absolutely true," Luisa said waspishly. "You let Marietta get away with far too much, Mamma."

"Why don't you just pack up your bags and wriggle back to that poor husband of yours?" Marietta suggested.

"Shut up, all of you!" Doucetta demanded. "A sick old lady like me, and you're fighting like a couple of alley cats. Shame on you. You especially, Luisa. What are you doing here? You should by home

281

with that bad-tempered husband of yours. You're here, instead, tormenting me! And look at you! In your nightgown at eleven o'clock in the morning. I want you dressed and out of my house! Go! Go!"

Luisa fled the room with a sob. Doucetta muttered angrily to herself. Then she said, "So, Mr. Fancy-Pants Detective. Will you find out why I am cursed?"

"I'll do what I can, Mrs. Capretti."

"Swear to me that you will find this killer!"

I cleared my throat. Then I said, "Yes, indeed."

"Murderers all around me," she grumbled. "The milk inspector? Someone did us all a favor there. The tax man? Pft." She spat. "No loss to the troops. But my buildings! My creamery! All my cheese!" The tears rolled down her cheeks. It was really quite horrible. "Aaaahhh!" she wailed.

"You really need to sit back and calm down, Grandmamma." Marietta sorted through the assorted detritus on the nightstand and held up a carafe. She glanced at me. "You don't think it's too early to give her a little red wine?"

It is a curious fact that some people see little difference between vets and physicians. "I see no harm in it all. As a matter of fact, I wouldn't mind some myself."

"Good idea." Marietta unearthed three glasses and poured a healthy slug of wine in each. I sat on the bed to drink it. Marietta sat next to me. She raised her glass. "To the goats," she said. "To the goats," Doucetta and I responded. The wine went down quite easily, being a cabernet franc of no small distinction, so we had another. It was quite cozy.

"Austin!" Madeline walked into the bedroom and stopped short. "Whatever are you doing?"

THIRTEEN

"You were cuddlin' her," Madeline said firmly.

"I was not," I said, just as firmly.

Madeline placed a dish of brown rice on the table and followed it with a plate of lima beans, corn, sliced red pepper, and chopped celery. I loathe lima beans. And brown rice sticks in my teeth.

"This is lunch?" I asked.

"It's a very healthy lunch. Practically no cholesterol at all."

I'd let Rita know I'd be leaving the dairy with my wife, and the two of us left Marietta to her grandmother and Luisa to her packing. Madeline had been very quiet on the ride home, except to remind us we were due in Hemlock Falls within the hour. She was quiet as she prepared lunch, and quiet until she sat down to eat it.

"Cuddlin'," she said again.

In twenty-two years of happily married

life, I have learned sometimes the best tactic is to suck it up. "If I were cuddling, it was inadvertent."

"That's worse."

"I apologize. Abjectly and sincerely. You are the light of my life, Madeline. I love you deeply. Marietta means nothing to me."

Madeline blinked. Her sapphire eyes were swimming. "You don't know just how attractive you are, Austin. Even at seventy-two. I'm sorry I hollered in front of everybody."

"It cheered Doucetta right up," I said ruefully. "She laughed so hard I thought we'd have to send her back to the ER."

Two dimples appeared in Madeline's cheeks. "She did, didn't she? Poor old thing. She's been through hell, right enough. And if it isn't enough that the dairy's in such a mess, she's got Luisa pitching around the house like a boat without a rudder." She got up and kissed me and sat down again. "I'm sorry I got a little ratty."

Suddenly, the lima beans didn't seem so awful. I swallowed a forkful. "I am very glad we aren't on the outs, my dear."

"Keep your hands off good-looking women and it won't happen again."

"Yes, my dear. Shall we go on to happier topics?"

"More useful ones, anyway. We've got this arson to solve on top of the murders."

"I understand you organized the volunteers in the goat sheds this morning. Who was there?"

"It was heartwarming to see how many people showed up to help. People you'd never expect. Rudy and Deirdre were there. And the mayor, although you'd expect that, this being an election year. And Swinford and Ashley showed up. They'll all have to come back day after tomorrow, of course, so we can give the does a second injection. But it went pretty well."

"Were any of the volunteers at the fire last night?"

She shook her head.

"Are you sure?"

"Pretty sure. If you'd like me to check, Trudy kept a list so that Marietta or whoever could send out thank-you notes. You want me to find out?"

"I think it would be helpful." I sat musing for a moment.

Madeline cleared the platters of rice and beans from the table. Then she sat and pushed her hands through her hair. "What a disaster for the dairy! Who could have done such a thing? And why?"

"Greed. Lust. Revenge," I said.

"I wish you wouldn't keep saying that," she said crossly. "You sound like something out of Edgar Allan Poe." She closed her eyes briefly. "There I go, snapping at you again. It's all this awful stuff. I feel so sorry for that old lady I could cry. Austin, we just have to find out who did this!"

"Yes," I said. I pushed the lima beans around my plate with my fork. "This is a curious case, my dear. Every likely suspect has a substantiated alibi. The Celestine brothers didn't get into the country until after the murders occurred. Their father spends his evening drunk as a skunk — in front of witnesses! The barn staff seems to go everywhere together and alibi each other. The only suppliers who have a grudge are in their eighties and wouldn't squash a fly if it flew up their respective noses."

"There's the cheese people."

"I had intended to go to Folk's office at the town hall and see if I can find any leads to the cheese people."

"I don't believe for a minute in the cheese people theory," Madeline said. "For one thing, if the cheese people want to buy out the dairy, they'd want the price as low as it can go, right? So the fire's to their advantage. But they seem to have hired Folk to be their go-between and here's Folk trying to get Melvin to give them a clean bill of health. I don't get it."

"That's easily explainable. Folk was undoubtedly getting a finder's fee if the deal went forward. And the fee is usually based on the percentage of the sale. It's a motivator to keep the assessment high, as well. If Folk were alive, I wouldn't find it totally unbelievable that he set the fire to force Doucetta to sell. But he's not. Perhaps an agent of his?" I bit my mustache. "I need to check Folk's office out. With luck, he kept an appointment book and I can track down who's behind the spurned offer to buy Tre Sorelle. There's one other suspect that we must consider, however. You realize that Neville was on the scene last night? Just before the fire started?"

Madeline put her hand to her cheek in dismay. "So that's what Doucetta was on about. Luisa's left Neville? And you're back to thinking he's behind this? No! I refuse to believe he had anything to do with it."

"There are laws of probability at work here, my dear. Do you really suppose that the murders and the fire are totally unrelated? What is most obvious is usually true. Neville is the only person connected with the dairy that had a motive to kill Staples that does not have an alibi. For either murder. I'm sure that Folk was at the dairy at the time of the murder, and that it can be verified. It is probable that he saw Neville kill Staples. And Neville is in a rage about his wife. He may have turned that rage toward the dairy itself."

"And Caterina was behind the sabotage of the milk." Madeline shook her head. "Which explains everything, at least. I don't know if it's right, though. It can't be! This is just awful."

I pushed myself away from the table. "I need to see Simon. I must gain access to Folk's files. And it's time Neville and I had another talk. And, of course, there's the question about the financial viability of the enterprise, especially now that the does are down for five months. I don't mean to press you, my dear, but we have a lot to do today. Are you ready to go to Hemlock Falls?"

The village of Hemlock Falls lies southeast of Ithaca, in the middle of the gorges. It is a spectacular drive from Summersville, even in the depths of winter. In summertime, it is glorious. For the half hour it took us to drive down 96, the green fields of corn, lush hedgerows, and the ponds of lichen-rich water drove all thoughts of murder from our minds.

Most of the buildings that sit on Main

Street in Hemlock Falls are constructed of stone quarried from the surrounding hills. The village must have a very active chamber of commerce; white stone planters filled with geraniums sat under wrought-iron lampposts and the signs on all the stores were of a consistent, attractive design.

"There's Thelma's car," Madeline said. A green Taurus was parked in front of a three-story stone building with a sign that said Nickerson's Hardware. "The store she wants is between the hardware store and that realty company."

"Schmidt's Realty Company and Casualty Insurance," I read aloud. I pulled in next to the Taurus and turned off the ignition. "What happened to the Hummer?"

"Leased, thank goodness. Thelma drove it right back to the showroom and stood there hollerin' until he cancelled the lease."

I shuddered. At full volume, Thelma's voice would rout the entire string section of the New York Philharmonic.

There was a small store tucked between the tall hardware building and the one-story stone affair that housed the realty company. A tall, handsome young man stood in the doorway. He looked part Indian to me; I learned later that he was half Onondaga. He looked down at us with a smile as Madeline and I approached him.

"Dr. McKenzie, Mrs. McKenzie?"

"We are," I said.

He extended his hand and shook ours in turn. "John Raintree. Mrs. Bergland and Dr. Bergland are inside."

"I'll go right in, sweetie. You stay out here and talk to Mr. Raintree." Madeline disappeared into the interior.

"It looks like a suitable space," I said. Cases Closed's first case had taught me that a few preliminary social niceties often pave the way to more productive questioning. I was not in the habit of being rude (as Victor had it) or too direct (as Ally said) or even insensitive (Who else but Madeline?). It was more a matter of wasting time in blather. But blather worked.

Raintree looked at the façade. "It's been through a number of incarnations. A Laundromat, a small restaurant, a woman's gym, a computing company."

I frowned a little. "It seems odd that a viable business wouldn't work here."

"The location's great," he said. "Other factors came into play. Not related to business."

Raintree had a restful quality about him. We stood in amiable silence for a while.

"Thelma's told you of her plan to open a

cheese store?"

He nodded thoughtfully. "Retail's never easy. But she's got the financial resources. The deeper the pocket the better."

"I understand you represent the Tre Sorelle Dairy?"

"Yes. Well, my firm does. I have a very good young CPA who's a wizard with Mrs. Capretti. I'm thinking of assigning him to Mrs. Bergland."

"A CPA with tact and charm, I gather," I said. We exchanged sapient glances. "You won't handle the account yourself, then?"

"Well, no," he said easily. "My expertise lies in handling larger companies. I'm glad I happened to be on hand to meet Mrs. Bergland, though. My wife and I are here to visit some old friends."

I was quite impressed. Mr. Raintree was the head of a successful firm and he had made that clear with tact and discretion.

"You're a veterinarian, Dr. McKenzie." He made this a statement of fact, rather than a question. "How much of an effect will the fire have on the dairy's operations?"

"Devastating," I said shortly. I explained about the necessity to rebreed the does. "Can the dairy survive?" I asked.

He didn't reply for a long moment. "I wouldn't advise anyone to invest in a dairy the size of Tre Sorelle," he said, finally. "The overhead's too high for the gourmet cheese business. You need does that produce year-round. You can't afford any drying up. And the number of milking does is too low for the high-volume, lower-quality cheese market." He smiled. "It's like the Three Bears story I tell my daughter at bedtime."

"If Mrs. Capretti were to receive an offer to buy her out, would you advise her to take it?"

"Mrs. Capretti has received such an offer. She turned it down." He looked at me, a frown of worry between his eyes. "The money's coming from somewhere," he said with sudden candor. "I don't know where. I have an idea. And if I'm right, we'll be resigning the account."

"I see," I said, although I didn't. Not yet. But if the same idea was nudging John Raintree into withdrawing his accounting services, it would explain a great deal about the murders.

What kind of trouble were the Celestine boys in when they were sent off to Italy?

Who were Doucetta's brothers, Pete and Tony's "wizard uncles"?

How "connected" was *Donna* Doucetta?

And why had the boys returned now?

"Dr. McKenzie?"

John Raintree's pleasant baritone jerked me out of my brown study. Two women had appeared out of nowhere and were smiling at me. The younger was tall, slender, with striking red hair and tea-colored eyes. The older one looked a bit like a Sherman tank, with ginger hair and a gaze as direct as a gunshot. "I beg your pardon. I was mulling over a small problem."

"Marge Schmidt," the tank woman said. "I own the store, here. You thinking about taking a lease?"

"Of Schmidt's Realty, of course," I said, shaking her hand. "I am not, but my wife and her friend Mrs. Bergland are considering it. They are inside."

"Hang on, Quill, John," Mrs. Schmidt said. "I'll be right out." She marched into the store.

"I'm Sarah McHale," her companion said. "Please call me Quill. And welcome to Hemlock Falls." She had a lovely voice.

The talk drifted into other channels, and I got no more tantalizing information from John Raintree. Thelma, Victor, and Madeline emerged from the prospective cheese store a short time later. We made our farewells, and Madeline and I were on our way back home.

"Thelma met her match in Marge

Schmidt," Madeline said. "But I think they came to an agreement about the lease. And how did you do, sweetie? Did John Raintree have anything interesting to say?"

I share everything with my wife. But I was not about to share my suspicions about the origins of the money that seemed to be keeping Tre Sorelle afloat. There was an element of danger there. "There might be a lead or two worth pursuing. But there are other matters of more urgency. I am going to go into Summersville to see Simon, and perhaps get more information on Brian Folk. May I drop you at home and use your car?"

"You go right on ahead, sweetie." She smiled at me. "You just sit on any impulse you might have to hug good-looking women!"

My tête-à-tête with Marietta was not soon to be forgotten.

Madeline's Prius was the only vehicle available to me since Joe and Allegra needed the Bronco for the Longacre farm call. The weather had become hotter and muggier. I left poor Lincoln at his post under the willow tree and drove the short distance into town. I was fortunate to find Provost, although he was on his way out the door when I walked into his office. He didn't look like a happy man. When he saw me, he looked unhappier. "There you are, Doc."

"I see I've caught you on the fly."

"What?" He stared at the car keys in his hand. "Yeah. So you did. It'll keep for a bit." He settled on the corner of his desk and punched a call into his intercom. "Kevin? I'm going to be another twenty minutes. Whyn't you go over to the sub shop and pick me up an Italian. No, not an Italian."

"The Bomber," I advised. The lima beans I had for lunch were a distant memory. "And I'd be much obliged if he would pick one up for me."

"You got that, Kevin? Two Bombers. And a couple of Diet Pepsis." He waved me toward the office chair. "You find out anything at the dairy this morning?"

"Not a lot that would be germane at the moment," I said evasively. "Did the arson team offer any preliminary results?"

He rubbed his chin. He'd been in a rush shaving that morning, for his chin was patchy with stubble. "Uh-huh. The gas bombs were made with wine bottles stuffed with T-shirts soaked with gasoline."

"That narrows the field considerably."

He grinned reluctantly. "Yep. I don't suppose there's a household in the United States of America that doesn't have two out of three on hand at any moment of the day."

"Any prints? Any torn labels? I don't suppose the arsonist left a driver's license tucked in a convenient spot?"

"Might as well have."

I raised my eyebrows. "There was a print on a glass shard?"

"Shard," Provost mused. "Where do you get these words, Doc?"

"There was a print on the glass shard and you already have a result."

"That team's amazing," Provost said with sincere admiration. "They have a scanner dingus attached to the computer, and as long as the prints are in the system, you get the answer right there at the site."

"Well?" I said impatiently. Suddenly, I knew. "Brandstetter."

Provost nodded, a short, abrupt nod that somehow conveyed how sorry he was.

"You realize that Neville is a Hoffmann Fellow, a PhD graduate of UC Davis, a tenured professor of repute at our veterinary school, which is the finest in the country, and he is not so stupid as to leave a fingerprint at the scene of a crime!"

"Don't shout, Doc. I can hear you just fine."

I hadn't realized I had risen out of my

chair. I sat back down again. "This is nonsense."

"Mrs. Brandstetter . . ."

"She is a fool and a hysteric," I said rudely.

"Mrs. Brandstetter confessed . . ."

"She cannot confess to something someone else did."

"Right you are. Mrs. Brandstetter told me that they got into a big argument over her messing around with Staples. She told him she was going back home to Mamma. She says he yelled at her if she did that, he'd burn the place down. . . ."

"Hyperbole."

". . . And it did. Burn down, I mean." He looked up as Kevin came in the door, two large submarine sandwiches in one hand and a pair of covered cups in the other. Kevin set them down on Provost's credenza and eyed me a little nervously. "We still on to go out to the suspect's house, Lieutenant?"

"There's no need to mince words, young man," I snapped. "I can tell you right now that Dr. Brandstetter is innocent."

"In a minute, Kevin. You go and start the report on the fire." Provost handed the sandwich over to me. "Eat this. Maybe your blood sugar's low or something. You can't tell me Brandstetter hasn't crossed your mind. What's the statistic on murder?"

"Most of the time it's a family member," I admitted. "Just not this time."

"Why are you so sure?"

I bit into the sub while I considered the question. "It seems to me that two types of people commit arson. Pyromaniacs. Habitual criminals. Brandstetter's neither. It's a horrific act, Provost. I admit, I can see Neville — any of us, as a matter of fact — pushed to the limit and killing someone on a furious impulse, as may have been the case with Staples. I can even see a desperate man nerving himself to kill again, to save himself, which could explain Folk's death. But to set a fire in a barn full of animals, with a ninety-four-year-old woman at risk, not to mention a number of other innocents? No. That's the act of a madman or a sadist."

Provost finished the last of his sandwich, balled up the paper wrapping, and threw it toward the wastebasket. It missed. "I've got to go where the evidence takes me, Austin. We can place him at the scene. He made the threat. His fingerprints were on the busted glass."

"Did you get the report back on Doucetta's cane?" I asked abruptly.

"Yeah, I did, as a matter of fact. It wasn't the murder weapon."

"Hm," I said.

"You're disappointed?"

"Yes. It would be almost impossible for Neville to get his hands on it long enough to commit either murder. It would have helped his defense. She had it with her almost constantly. And will again if you get it back to her."

"It's not evidence anymore." He pointed at the top of his filing cabinet. The cane lay across it, no longer encased in plastic. "You can take it back to her if you'd like."

I rose and picked it up. "I'll do that. Do you have any idea what was used?"

"Who knows, Doc? A blunt instrument like that could be almost anything."

"It is not 'almost anything,'" I said testily. "The autopsy report was quite specific." I waved it at him. "A long-handled instrument with a bulbous top. Probably made of metal. That doesn't sound like the typical blunt instrument to me, Simon."

"You have a point. But it's not necessary evidence in this kind of case."

"You have absolutely no reason to make that assumption." I folded my arms and leaned back against the wall. Now was not the time to discuss my suspicions about the new direction the case had taken. I had one insurmountable problem. And because of it, Simon would dismiss my speculation as just that: conjecture. And it was the problem that had plagued the case from the beginning. No one could have done it. Everyone had an alibi.

"You about through ranting?" Provost eased himself off the desk. "I'm going to pick him up now." He held up his hand. "Don't even think about asking to come with me. Thank God Mrs. Brandstetter's over at her mother's. I've never heard such a racket from any woman the last time I took Brandstetter in. You know I had to bring him down here for the first interview. I couldn't hear myself think with all that shrieking going on."

I looked at my watch. "Hard luck, Provost. Doucetta threw her out this morning. If you hurry, you'll catch her walking in the door."

Provost seriously considered taking a policewoman to aid in Brandstetter's arrest. I left him mulling over tactics and walked across the street to the town hall. It was past time to look into Brian Folk's affairs.

Summersville grew up as an exurb around the universities in the late twenties and thirties. We have a few fine old cut-stone buildings. The *Summersville Sentinel* is housed in one and the town hall is in another. The high ceilings and the terrazzo flooring keep the building quite cool in the summer. Although a few offices were air-conditioned, the building as a whole was not.

The tax assessor's office is on the second floor. I found a harried young woman putting files into cardboard boxes. She jerked up with a shriek when I tapped on the open door to announce my presence. "Good grief! You scared the living daylights out of me." She had a soft, pudgy face, lovely skin, and brown hair in a long, sloppy ponytail down her back.

"My apologies," I said. It was warm in the office. The window was open to the street outside. "I'm Austin McKenzie." I tucked Doucetta's cane under my arm and held out my hand.

"Mary Ellen Lochmeyer." She wiped her sweaty palm on her jeans and shook my hand. "I'm the assistant."

"Assistant what?"

"Just assistant. Right now, it's assistant to the tax assessor's office because he's dead. I sort of float, if you know what I mean. The council sends me all over the place. Like the Highway Department. I was assigned there for a couple of weeks because all these guys took vacation all at once. It was a nightmare. And I help out at the county clerk's office when justice court's in session."

She was a chatterer. In the years I've supervised students, I've had more than one. There is nothing for it but to rudely interrupt the flow. "I've just come from Lieutenant Provost."

"The police?" she said. "I was assigned to the dispatcher's desk once for a couple of days. It was kind of fun. But the real dispatcher came back, worse luck."

"I'm here for Brian Folk's Day-Timer, I believe it's called."

"You mean his calendar? Nobody uses Day-Timers anymore."

"Whatever he used to keep his appointments."

She sighed. "You're from the police?"

"I've just come from the police lieutenant's office," I said. I admit to being Jesuitical. But it was literally true. If necessary, I was prepared to pull out my honorary deputy ID.

She set the box she held onto the desk with an irritated thump. She thumbed rapidly through a pile of papers and held out a John Deere wall calendar. "He used this. He probably had a BlackBerry, too, but I imagine that was on him when he was, you know, killed." After a moment she added, "Poor guy."

I flipped through May, June, and July. As I thought, he was a methodical man. One cannot perform what is essentially an accounting function otherwise. The squares allocated to weekdays were divided in half. The word "county" was neatly printed in most of the spaces above the line. The lower half held afternoon appointments.

"Find something weird?" Mary Ellen asked.

"Something that should have occurred to me by now," I said. "I will need to keep this."

She held her hand out. "Then I'll need a receipt."

"I don't have my receipt book on me," I confessed.

"Policemen always carry a book of receipts. It's so they can legally acquire evidence when necessary. I learned that when I was assisting at the county clerk's office." She squinted at me. "Hey. Aren't you kind of old to be a policeman? No offense," she added hastily.

"I'll make out a receipt," I said. "Give me that pad of paper, please." I took a pen and scribbled:

Received from Mary Ellen Lochmeyer one calendar belonging to Brian Folk. 7.8.07. And signed it *Austin McKenzie, DVM (Deputy).*

She took the paper, read it, and shook her head. "It's not July eighth. It's August seventh."

"I know perfectly well what day it is," I said testily. "That is the European method of writing dates. You put the day first and then the mo—" I stopped in midsentence and stared at her. "My God. Of course. That's it."

"That's what?"

"That's it!"

"Hey!" she called after me as I exited the office and walked rapidly down the hall. "Aren't you Dr. McKenzie? That vet that writes that column with all the gruesome stuff that can happen to your dog?"

I waved the cane over my shoulder without turning around and exited the building to Main. I got into the Prius and sat there, considering my next move.

Brian Folk had spent a lot time with Jonathan Swinford. I disliked the man — but I failed to see him as a member of the kind of organized crime that I suspected supported the dairy.

It was time to have a serious talk with Doucetta Capretti.

FOURTEEN

Evening was coming on as I drove into the courtyard of the Tre Sorelle Dairy. There was a soft murmur of goats in the air. A crew of workers cleared the stinking remnants of the milking parlor into huge Dumpsters. Tony and Pete were at the office door, at work replacing the fallen sconce.

At the sound of my arrival, Caterina came out onto the step, a thermos of coffee in one hand and a plate of coffee cake in the other. It was a peaceful, busy scene, as unlike the chaos of the morning as could be imagined.

I raised my hand in salute. Tony grinned and waved, and I made my way toward them.

"Back again, Doc?" Pete asked. He put a final screw in the wall and tightened the sconce bracket with a grunt. It was made of iron, long, with a bulbous top.

"That ought to stay up for a while," I said

approvingly. "You'll make sure it does?"

"Huh?"

"Sorry. My wife tells me I can be a bit overbearing. I like to see a job well done, however. And yes, I'm back again. I have a few questions for your grandmother. And of course, there's this." I rapped the flagstone with the goat-headed cane.

"She's going to be some kind of flipped out to see that," Tony said. "So the lab guys cleared it, huh? That's not what helped Mel and Folk out of this world and into the next?"

My glance rested on the sconce. "No."

"Mamma's up at the house," Caterina said. She raised the tray of coffee cake with an inquiring lift of her eyebrows. I declined with a gesture. "Marietta's keeping an eye on her."

"And how are the goats?"

"Seem to be fine," Caterina said. "Ashley didn't make it in to work today, so I entered all the data about the stock myself." She took a deep, prideful breath. "And we're handling the second set of injections tomorrow all by ourselves, Dr. McKenzie. We aren't going to need all those volunteers at all."

"Take it easy, Ma," Pete said. Her put his arm around her shoulders and squeezed her close. "One step at a time, here."

She beamed up at him, her face bright with maternal feeling.

I made my way up the flagstone steps to the house and rang the doorbell. Marietta opened it almost at once. "I saw you come in," she said. "You got it back! She's going to be so pleased. Follow me. We're out on the terrace having a glass of wine."

She walked through the magnificent house to the terrace overlooking the lake. Doucetta sat in a rocking chair, her eyes on the horizon. The setting sun sent streaks of mauve and purple through the orangey sky.

Doucetta seized her goat-headed cane like a ewe discovering a lost lamb. "Thank God. And the Virgin. The curse is lifted."

Marietta rolled her eyes. But she smiled and gave her grandmother a hug. "You bet the curse is lifted. It's all uphill from here."

"I wouldn't be too sure about that," I said gravely. "May I sit down?"

"Of course! Please!" Marietta pulled a wrought-iron chair forward. "We love to sit out here in the evenings. The setting sun makes the sky so beautiful. Times like this, I don't miss the city so much."

"The color comes from pollution," I observed. "But it is spectacular."

"Hm." Marietta took a sip from a glass of

the wine that had gotten me into trouble with my wife. She waved the glass at me. "Sure I can't get you some?"

"I'm certain, thank you." I was to need all my wits about me. "Marietta, Lieutenant Provost is in the process of arresting Neville for the murders."

She set the glass down and looked at me, wide-eyed. "No! Neville did it?"

"There is quite a bit of evidence against him. But no, Neville didn't do it."

"You seem awfully sure about that. I mean, Summersville's a bit of a backwater, but I always thought Simon Provost was one smart cop."

Doucetta sat with both feet firmly planted on the flagstone, her cane between her knees, and her hands folded over the brass goat's head on the top. She looked at me for a long time, her gaze direct, unwinking, and cold. "My son-in-law didn't do it," she said flatly.

"No, Mrs. Capretti."

Marietta looked from one of us to the other. "You both sound as if you know who did."

This was the tricky part. Simon had read the passport entry date wrong. It wasn't August sixth that the young assassins had entered the country, but June eighth. The

European style of writing calendar dates is the reverse of the American method. They had been in the United States for two full months before emerging into the public eye. They had no alibi for murder. And Doucetta knew it.

"They are my family," she said to me.

"In more ways than one, I expect, *Donna* Doucetta." I placed a great deal of emphasis on the honorific. She blinked once. Then a reluctant smile spread over her face, and she made a rumbling, choking sound that came from deep inside her chest. I looked at Marietta in alarm. She in turn gazed at her grandmother with exasperation.

"What's so funny, Grandmamma?"

She jerked her thumb at me. "Him. He thinks I am of the Black Hand. He thinks I am a female don. Hahahahahaha." The laugh stopped as abruptly as it started. "No, arsehole. I am not." She sighed heavily and repeated. "I am not. But my poor grandsons. That may be another story." She passed her hand over her face, as if erasing any feeling that might show there. "Ah. It's a good thing your poor grandfather isn't alive."

"I am totally confused here," Marietta said sharply.

"It's probably best that you remain that way, cousin." Tony stepped onto the terrace.

His teeth were very white in his suntanned face. His brother followed him onto the terrace. The two of them went to the balustrade and leaned against it, facing us.

Caterina came from the depths of the house. She carried a tray filled with cheese, olives, and salami. She bumped the doors open with her hip, brought the tray through, and set it on the round table. The wind picked up her graying hair and she moved her bangs off her forehead with one hand. She handed me a small plate and a cocktail napkin. "The boys said you found out about the sconce."

"Pure happenstance," I said. "It's quite logical as a weapon. I was remiss in overlooking it. It was at hand. And, like the Purloined Letter, you were able to hide it in plain sight."

Tony mimed swinging a baseball bat.

"Arrete!" Doucetta said.

"Sorry," Tony said.

"So what's next, *donna?*" Pete said.

"What's this?" Marietta demanded. "What's going on here?" She put her hands on her hips and glared at her aunt. "Caterina! What's this all about? Are you saying . . ." She faltered. "Tony and Pete. Did they . . ." She took a huge breath and sat down as though her legs had been knocked out from under her.

Doucetta stood up, stamped over to her daughter, and spat on the ground at her feet. "You tried to kill the dairy. You tried to kill me!"

"Oh, stuff it, Mamma. You just can't accept the fact that it's over. When you turned down the offer from Swinford's firm, that was the last straw." She pushed impatiently at her hair. "Five million dollars for this place. You were a fool not to take it. Well, all I can say is, you're going to have to take it now. You can't survive five months. It's done. Finished. Over." She smiled. "Now *that's* an inheritance."

"I am not dead yet," Doucetta said. "I will cut you off without a penny!"

"No, you won't." Caterina put her hand under her mother's elbow and escorted her back to her chair. "We're family. You'd rather cut off your right arm than cut us off." Her lips drew back, and for a moment, the pleasant, downtrodden woman I knew looked wolfish. "Even Frank, right? You made me stick with him all these years because our family doesn't divorce." The look passed. Her face sagged back into the tired lines of a middle-aged woman. "So don't talk to me about being cut out of the will."

"Don't be so sure about that," the old woman grumbled.

Caterina knelt by her mother's chair. "The dairy can't keep itself, Mamma. The only thing keeping us afloat is the money that goes through the retail store on behalf of the Italian uncles. And we're going to have to stop that. Banking's tightened up so much after 9/11 we can't get the money in and out liked we used to. It's time to let go."

Doucetta reared back as if she'd been stung. "What are you telling me, here!"

"You really thought we were making it without help from the uncles?"

Marietta clutched her forehead in both hands and sank her head onto her knees. "I don't believe this," she said. "Money laundering? Murder? And we've got — connected uncles?"

Doucetta smacked her cane point-down on the concrete. *"Basta!"* she shouted. "You've ruined us all! And you've betrayed me!"

"We'll be fine if you don't panic," Caterina said. "And think of the money coming in from the cheese people. That'll go a long way toward making up for the betrayal."

"You didn't have to burn the place down to convince me!"

"We'd tried everything else." She clasped her mother's hands. "Okay? Is it all okay?"

Doucetta mumbled her lips. And she looked very, very old. Ancient. Like something that had been exhumed. She nodded once, sharply.

Caterina stood up and looked at her sons. "Now. As for Dr. McKenzie."

Her sons turned and looked at me.

The wind off the lake was suddenly cold.

"Don't you dare," Marietta said between her teeth. She looked up at them. "Don't even think about it."

"Think about what?" Pete said.

Tony mimed swinging a baseball bat.

"If you touch a hair on his head," Marietta said dramatically, "you will have to go through me."

"I never liked the smell of goat," Marietta complained.

"The bucks do have a repellant odor," I admitted. "But the does are quite neat in their habits and odor free."

We were tied together, sitting back-to-back in the dairy nursery. This was a room about fifteen by twenty feet long, located at the rear of the principal goat shed. The lights were on, in an effort to promote rapid estrus in the does. There was a large viewing window on one side, and an overhead door at the rear. Directly in front of us were overhead feeders loaded with hay. The vista out the viewing window was pitch black. The overhead door was locked. The five does and eight newborn kidlings who were the legitimate residents of the pen lay comfortably in the straw. The mothers chewed their cuds and looked blandly at us. Goats have vertical pupils, and their eyes can appear quite human. It was actually quite comforting, as if little people stared warmly at us. The babies suckled, slept, and occasionally tumbled over one another like newborn puppies. . . .

"What time is it?" Marietta asked, for perhaps the hundredth time. . . . The woman was becoming tiresome. She had discovered I was able to twist my wrist to look at my watch and asked every half hour or so. "Three thirty," I said. "I suggested that you try and get some sleep. I'll suggest it again. The barn help won't be in to feed and water until six at least."

Marietta wriggled in the straw, trying to find a more comfortable spot. She'd wriggled so much when Tony and Pete dumped us in here that she'd worn a bare spot right to the dirt floor.

"Where do you suppose they're going, the

three of them?"

"I have no idea." Actually, I did have an idea. I had lost my pension fund in the Enblad scandal several years ago. The CFO was currently living on an island with no extradition treaty to the United States. "It may be somewhere in the Pacific. Or, perhaps even Italy itself. That country refuses to extradite criminals to countries with the death penalty."

"Do you suppose the cheese people will still want to buy us?"

"If your grandmother agrees, I don't see why not." I paused. "You were dealing with Jonathan Swinford, weren't you?"

"Yes! How did you know that? He didn't want the news to get out until the deals were done. Can't say as I blame him. The vineyard's part of DairyMaid now. It's publically traded, as you probably know, and they have to be cautious about the stock."

"I deduced as much. But why did he choose Brian Folk as an intermediary?"

"Beats me. Folk wasn't stupid. Just icky-looking."

"Icky-looking." I laughed heartily. Marietta laughed, too.

The lights outside the viewing window snapped on. I saw a furry, familiar face at the window. The air filled with loud barks.

"Lincoln!" I said.

A few moments later the overhead door to the nursery rolled up. My wife swept into the room.

"Austin!" she said. "What in the world do you think you're doing?"

"You're darn lucky you weren't killed," Victor said. "Good God, Austin. You should think seriously about giving up the detective business."

I passed the plate of beer-battered onion rings over to Joe. "Yes, indeed. Tied up for hours in a darkened room with Marietta Capretti. Very dangerous."

We exchanged a long, wordless look.

"I'm shocked to my bones," Thelma said. "Just imagine. Organized crime right here in Summersville!"

"It's a heck of a story," Rita said proudly.

We had persuaded Rudy Schwartz to push together three tables in the center of the Monrovian Embassy, to celebrate the successful conclusion of the Case of the Ill-Gotten Goat. Madeline had lifted the ban on cholesterol, and I had a huge Monrovian Special in front of me. Allegra, Joe, Nigel Fish (whose besotted expression when he looked at Allegra reminded me of a flounder), and Rita sat on one side of the long table. Madeline, Thelma, Victor, and I sat on the other. My happiness would have been complete had Lincoln been allowed to join us, but Rudy was unfeelingly obdurate.

"Anyone figure out where Caterina and her sons got to?" Joe asked.

"Last the Feds heard, they were on a plane out of La Guardia headed to South America," Nigel said. "They must have had an exit plan in place. They sure made it out of town in a hurry."

"What do you suppose is going to happen to that five million dollars Doucetta's going to get from the cheese people?" Allegra asked. "Do you think she'll use the money to open a boutique dairy?"

"She'll have quite a competitor in me," Thelma said immodestly. "I signed the lease on my new store today."

"Really?" Joe said. "You decide what to call it?"

"Madeline suggested the name. I think it's perfect. I'm calling it Le Grand Fromage."

There was a moment of silence.

"Because," Thelma said with immense satisfaction, "I am."

COTTAGE CHEESE RECIPE

Cheese is easy to make! Austin talked Madeline into trying this recipe for cottage cheese. It makes a wonderful cheese cake.

1 gallon goat milk★
1/4 tablet rennet, sometimes called junket
1/2 cup cold water

1. Use a kitchen thermometer to warm the milk to 86°F.
2. Dissolve the rennet in the water.
3. Add water/rennet mixture to the milk. Stir it up a little. Let it stand in a warm place (75°F or above) until a curd forms on the surface. This should take an hour or so.
4. Leave the mixture in the pot. Cut the curd into one-inch squares.
5. Stir gently.
6. Warm very slowly to 110°F.
7. Strain mixture into a sieve lined with

cheesecloth.

8. Rinse mixture by running cold water over it. (Don't remove it from the colander.)

9. Store in the refrigerator in a covered bowl.

This cottage cheese can be mixed with all kinds of delicious things: chopped chives, your favorite seasonings, chopped parsley, and salt. You can make it a sweet cottage cheese by adding honey or jam.

★ You can use cow's milk if all your goats are out to pasture.

AUTHOR'S NOTE

Goats are delightful pets — smart, sweet-natured, and kind. An excellent primer on goat care is *Storey's Guide to Raising Dairy Goats* by goat-keeper extraordinaire Jerry Belanger.

And for more cheese recipes, contact the New York State Farmstead and Artisan Cheese Makers Guild via their website.

For those readers interested in raising goats, there is an industry newspaper called the *Goat Rancher* that can be found online at www.goatrancher.com. It is there you will find outstanding editorials by our industry's guru, Frank Pinkerton, PhD, whom we call "The Goat Man."

ABOUT THE AUTHOR

Claudia Bishop is the pen name of Mary Stanton. She is the author of eighteen mystery novels. *The Case of the Ill-Gotten Goat* is Austin McKenzie's third case.

Claudia is also the senior editor of three mystery anthologies. As Mary Stanton, she is the author of two adult fantasy novels and eleven novels for middle-grade readers.

Claudia divides her time between a small home in West Palm Beach, Florida, and a two-hundred-acre goat farm in upstate New York. She can be reached through her website, claudiabishop.com.

The employees of Thorndike Press hope you have enjoyed this Large Print book. All our Thorndike and Wheeler Large Print titles are designed for easy reading, and all our books are made to last. Other Thorndike Press Large Print books are available at your library, through selected bookstores, or directly from us.

For information about titles, please call:
  (800) 223-1244

or visit our Web site at:
  http://gale.cengage.com/thorndike

To share your comments, please write:
  Publisher
  Thorndike Press
  295 Kennedy Memorial Drive
  Waterville, ME 04901